The Best of Bumpus

The Best of Bumpus

Fifteen Stories by Jerry Bumpus

Selected and Edited
by Duff Brenna

 Serving
House
Books

The Best of Bumpus

ISBN: 978-1-947175-00-6

Cover art by William Blake

Serving House Books logo by Barry Lereng Wilmont

Published by Serving House Books
Copenhagen, Denmark, Florham Park, NJ

www.servinghousebooks.com

Member of The Independent Book Publishers Association

First Serving House Books Edition 2018

To Bettie, my dear wife, and Margot, our dear daughter, and Peter Bumpus, our faithful puppy dog.

Books by Jerry Bumpus

Anaconda
Things in Place
Special Offer
Heroes and Villains
The Happy Convent
Dawn of the Flying Pigs
The Civilized Tribes
The Best of Bumpus

Contents

The Best of Bumpus

JERRY BUMPUS IS PROFESSOR EMERITUS at San Diego State University. He holds a BA in English from the University of Missouri, and an MFA in Creative Writing from the University of Iowa. He has published 121 stories, 24 of which have been anthologized. He has also published five story collections and two novels. His third novel has been brewed and is in the final stages of polishing. His work has appeared in *Esquire*, *The Paris Review*, *The Best American Short Stories* (1974 and 1975), *Tri-Quarterly*, *The Iowa Review*, and dozens of other respected journals.

In the fifteen stories comprising *The Best of Bumpus*, his sixth collection, he uses a writing tactic familiar to any fan following his work: Each story's setting is launched in a locale that is generally recognizable to an average reader, before eventually veering into what appear to be very tenuously attached sensibilities of actual life. Some of these conceptions have the dark nightmarish quality of a dreamer inhabiting a world that has no east or west, north or south, no up or down, but rather points of reference that are boundless, wherein what we witness is concrete, but also gelatinous. True, yes, but not exclusively true in a three-dimensional world. The darkness on display is often fragmented with slants of light through which one repeatedly experiences laugh-out-loud humor (usually as outlandish as it is ironic), unashamed sex of every imaginable type, and a tangible madness lying beneath the carapace humans wear as a means of survival. He uncovers and explores lives that cast a spell as real as voodoo to those who practice voodoo, or perhaps practice the enraptured cannibalism of eating a god transmogrified into a wafer. It can be grotesque; it can also be spellbinding, revealing an imagination frequently beyond description.

Bumpus' stories and novels model the weirdness of not just our species but all species of every sort. If a critic had to pick a dominant theme that the author obsessively explores, that theme might be: *life is absurd.* The absurdity of it all, the absurd nature of existence itself, the absurd behavior of human beings caught between the billions of years before life somehow arose, and the billions of years that will follow its extinction.

Paradigms: "Anaconda (An Excerpt)," wherein we meet Alonzo McCafferty, a wanderer *wandering* vaguely back in time. He doesn't know where he's going and only tentatively knows where he's been, though it all may be a dream he's dreaming on the move whose purpose will reveal itself if he just keeps going, perhaps to a setting that honors "Things in Place" which enters the point of view of a man named Haskel, a semi-hermit living in a canyon between "two buttes staring at each other." Haskel calls them "the Big Ideas" because "They looked sure of why they were there." Mid-story he meets Lily and Hopalong, two motorcycle gang members ejected from their tribe, their motorcycle long gone, along with Hopalong's penis.

Bumpus writes unlike anyone his readers are likely to know. He is flying millimeters above any "normal" plot with "normal" characters, on his own skewed trajectory (although here and there, as through the looking glass, one catches hints of Faulkner in the midst of devilishly creative word play, e.g. *The Sound and the Fury* or *Sanctuary*, that same masterful deftness, beauty and humor sporadically macabre, as in "Mrs. Bell and Her Dog," where Larry Tyler, a handicapped man (he may be a dwarf or a midget) has a room in a boarding house whose upstairs hall is patrolled at intervals by a menacing dog. "There was an awful beauty in the dog — a valueless beauty, amazing, based on its intensity, its brutal thoughtlessness, its great size." Mrs. Bell bullies the dog, and the dog bullies Larry. It sees and smells Larry's weakness—which is always a canine come on. Mrs. Bell takes pleasure in teasing the dog, yelling at it as she does at Larry. It's a distorted bestial marriage between her and the dog, with Larry as their child needing chastisement. The threesome illustrates a story of twisted persistence. There is no cunning involved; circumstance, inclination and/or fear drive the players forward. Terrifying Larry becomes the goal for both the old lady and her fanged monster.

Riveting and ruthless and rough and immoral might be a way of marketing what happens in "A Lament to Wolves." A clueless mother (is she really clueless?) seems to turn a blind eye to the fact that her son Loren is about to seduce his own sister Ella. He's been away for many years, but now that he's come home the desirable daughter becomes bait to keep him captivated. The self-deluded mother says to Ella, "Thank God the boy's turned out good. He's a good man, like his daddy was." Ella is staring numbly out the window as the mother continues, "It's a miracle ... If you ask me, it's a miracle of God," and then she goes silent, until "the nervous movement of her lips resumed, the restless whispering." Of course Loren is exactly like his daddy was, and therein rests the problem that not even Ella will admit to herself.

"The Angel Business" seems to take place on another planet that looks like Earth but spawns supernatural phenomenon such as angels who pester human beings, some who are as rapacious as the angels themselves. An old friend named Russell steps out of the past, arriving at the narrator's door and proceeding to take over his life. Soon there are eight guests having dinner at the house. As they sit at the table, Russell brings up the existence of "Angels ... big white angels." A guest named Koch asks him what he has by way of proof. Mrs. Russell rises and says, "We have a plethora of proof. Enlarged glands ..." "Photographs," Russell corrects her before she continues: "Enlarged photographs. Plaster casts of footprints. Large fingerprints which have no swirls or whorls" — she lifts her arm, her big hand spiraling upward. "And of course we have the best proof of all," Russell said. "The angels themselves." Servants wheel in a table bearing a display: a plaster print of a large, five-toed foot with a horn-like projection at the heel — a talon, Russell calls it. That night a "house angel" brings a clattering, shattering chaos that has some guests fleeing in terror. Others remain determined to capture the thing. Ultimately, *it* doesn't show up to be captured and we are left to consider whether Russell is a con man or an angel himself. And what of his supposed confederates? At first they seem to be a cabal hunched round a table at a séance, mesmerized by possibilities that might actually exist. Or are they merely dupes for one man's giant, self-absorbed ego?

"House Hunting Near the Frontier" creates a daydream of dark closets inside a crumbling home, where two parents and their young son wander aimlessly, while whispers fill the air. Ears cocked, the boy believes that his mother and father are talking about him. He knows that he is more of a nuisance than anything and no one knows what to do with him. Poe's "The Cask of Amontillado" comes to mind.

"Flowers in Your Hair" opens with a man lying in bed musing about a trip to San Francisco and wearing flowers in his hair. Someone lies beside him saying "Yes" to all he says as he ruminates about who or what he is.

He asks himself if the feeling he's experiencing is actually normal. A little matter of a pronoun gives the ending of this flash piece an unexpected twirl that makes everything surprisingly clear, Bumpus putting the end stop in just the right place as crafty writers frequently do.

"Dawn of the Flying Pigs" makes the point that an overabundance of male endowment (so much so that it causes "stunned fascination and frenzied adulation") may not be the gift that many men think it is. If you're too large down there and inclined to flaunt it, you may find your "gift" is actually a curse.

Two boys become "Chums" (sort of) when one leads the other to "a mausoleum as large as an apartment house, with barred windows set high in the walls, almost to the slate roof." Once inside the huge crypt, the first boy, "narrow-faced, yellow eyes, a V smile, his body like a stick," goes to a casket, climbs inside and invites the other boy to join him. What happens is revolting, yet transfixing and almost unbelievable, yet undeniably human, proving once again the species is capable of anything — anything that can be imagined, that is.

"Heroes and Villains" characterizes the wild imagination of a writer named Mirna who "was fairly sure this wasn't a dream she was having, though now in the gray gallery it all seemed tremendously far away." She has been distracted, in part, by a remarkable face she is either seeing or imagining, "yellow and protuberant as if his head had been squeezed from behind, bulging his eyes, jutting his lips, and creating at least a fistful of nose." Is she writing a story, or is she seeing something concrete? "Were they tumblers?" Mirna says aloud, visualizing a troupe of little people tumbling down a corridor, a white pony's hooves clattering, a calliope sending its hopeful tootle echoing through a hospital. "Tumblers?" a nurse named Hudlow says. "Ah — " rolling her eyes up — "no. More like actors. Actors being ordinary in gray suits. Ah — actors in politics, dicks and goons." Mirna walks down a hall, nurses walking on each side of her, and when she asks about her hospitalized daughter: "Is Eileen resting well?" The answer is: "She — ah — remains catatonic …That's resting very well." *What mysteries we are*, thinks Mirna.

The conversation (or hallucination) continues: "I guess you know they got the husband of that one," says a girl hiding in a corner and nodding toward Eileen on the bed. "Crunched him down to a bouillon cube. But my

Robert they sliced off half of him — the back half, from the head straight down. If he ever walks again he'll have to tiptoe everywhere — no heels."

In the next scene, Basil Stein (an undercover cop?) takes out a book called *We Wiser Disguisers*, reads a line or two, then looks up. "Why are you interfering in these affairs, my dear?" he asks. And Mirna tells him, "I happened to be in the country to see my publisher." Like actors playing the same part on or off stage, Mirna stays in role wherever she goes.

At a house and caught between two groups of men firing assault rifles at each other, Mirna sees "Through the dust" [the fog of war?], two black men stumbling through a kitchen and out the back door, carrying a washing machine with a chained woman riding on it. Next thing Mirna knows is that she is under the house hiding from the bullets flying above. Someone comes down and yells, "Everything's on fire!" "The floor was hot and through it they heard fire, a steady, increasingly loud rumble. "Dig!" Mirna yells as she claws the sand. "Roy dug beside her, scooping out sand between his legs like a dog. He shoved his face into the shallow hole, and cupped sand over his ears and neck. Mirna sees all the chaos as an enactment of what happened to Patty Hearst's kidnappers — the Symbionese Liberation Army with their hideout burning down around them. Later after escaping the horror, she finds a slim volume with a slick black cover. "She opened it and read the first lines, casually metered and rather obscure, rather private, concerning her life with heroes and villains."

The tendency for this reader was to follow the fantasy (if it is a fantasy) wherever Mirna's imagination was taking it. It's a *brilliant* story, maybe the most mesmerizing in an entire collection packed with riveting tales like "Lovers" demonstrating the destructive but innocent nature of children undisciplined and doing what a child might do if she or he were left to their own devices. It's possible that every neighborhood has a teenage girl who behaves like a lover named Penny, whose "reputation flowed from mouth to ear among boys close to her age." A girl who gives into the promptings of her maturing body, for which boys found in themselves the inchoate winds of change blowing them toward the "meaning of life," boys brave enough or entranced by the compelling nature of Penny girls.

A man and two women sit on a patio "shaded by the web of the biggest spider Charles has ever seen." When he offers to kill it with a board, Frankie says, "Go ahead," at the same time Ruth says, "No way! Mr. Spider is my buddy." It turns out that Ruth is the spider spinning a psychosomatic web around "Mr. Tangible," transfixing him before preparing to take him apart inch by inch.

Introducing "Patsy O'Day in the World," a young woman living an aimless life, call it a "hippie" existence where strangers, friends, and lovers come and go, none with a purpose that she can measure. Their bodies are open for whatever happens, no matter how absurd it might seem: a drug-addled, suicidal boy leaps out a window; people wander the streets throughout the night; couples make love without passion, not knowing each other's names. Patsy, an outsider in their midst, is peripatetic but going nowhere. There is nothing on her mind that she can name. It's all gray—the sky, the apartment, the suicidal boy's eyes, the landlord, no more Technicolor in a life she never chose for herself. One gray day following another surrounded by gray walls, gray people, rainy gray skies.

"You might think that since they were old hands as nurses they would have realized there prevailed a downward inevitability in things," but Hobart in "A Song of Old Fangles" saw in them "no more acceptance or wisdom than in other people, and certainly less inclination to accepting defeat." He falls for one of the nurses: "And she was huge. Her arms and legs bulged, and her hips were little people stowed away under her uniform, riding her through the night." "No false modesty," Mrs. Nash told Hobart. "You can whip anything. You know what?" She winks, "sending shivers through him as he stares at her face," a face "small and coy atop her big body." "I can tell about people," she says and licks her lips. Hobart is a good kid. Employees at the hospital where he works love that he's so kind and helpful. He has a wife who gives birth to a boy near the end of the story. It's a triumphant moment for Hobart—until it isn't.

Helen Droosman has a stroke. But she survives and eventually is well enough to go back to her real estate business. A man and woman show up one day wanting to see a house that has been advertised. Helen proudly calls it "A Very Modern Home." She makes an appointment to meet them the next day, but when she arrives, the couple isn't there. The mailbox is full, so she "starts taking the letters from the box when a woman opened the door" and Helen realizes she's at the wrong house. She makes the best of it. A small mistake, but how nice the woman is, smiling and nodding, understanding Helen's dilemma. Then suddenly the nice woman points past Helen's shoulder and says, "Is that your car going off by itself?" Indeed, the car canters down the street and bumps into a tree and "Water poured swiftly through her head," a phenomena that keeps occurring. Eventually, we understand the feeling of water is akin to a mini-stroke.

The next day, Helen meets the couple and drives them to the house, but she gets lost again and again, before finally finding the right address. Bumpus describes it: "… an enormous empty lot covered with trees and underbrush. But through the tangled landscaping gone wild they saw a high gray wall." Water pours through Helen's head again. She tries to lead the couple inside, but can't find the entrance. The husband, Mr. Taylor, finds the way in. Helen tries to lead, but she's soon lost and the couple go off by themselves, up stairways in and out of rooms, while Helen longs for something, a chair "or any kind of furniture" so she can sit down. What she finds is a huge white room, "the largest she had ever seen".

"A Very Modern Home" is as straightforward as user-friendly stories ever get. It stays firmly in Helen's mind and describes her medical condition so precisely that one might wonder if Bumpus has ever experienced what his character is experiencing in such unfocused yet extraordinary detail. To think that it may all be *imagined* is to leave one a little stunned and acutely awed.

The stories in *The Best of Bumpus* present their creator at his most accessible, least accessible, and accessible *maybe, maybe not.* That is to say: the Bumpus world is *bedrock real* one moment and *shifting sands unreal* on the page opposite, depending on the subject matter and who or what is narrating. Some characters have one foot in here-and-now certainties, while the other foot toes the lunacies of a dream, revealing tenuous connections between bizarre behavior and pure accident and the oddities of unforeseen collisions between minds conventional and minds caught in a maelstrom of what our lives can be — daily clutches of anxiety, angst, disbelief, fear, a sense of living in alternate dimensions — no bottom or walls or resting places, all of it seriously human and, by association, *absurd.* Look to Xanax. Pray for sleep.

Duff Brenna, 2018

ANACONDA (AN EXCERPT)

VERA HAD BEEN QUIET FOR A LONG TIME. She was on her fifth drink and was beginning to get a little maudlin. E.L. had started drinking again, but much slower than before. McCaferty kept up his steady pace with beer.

The girl looked sternly at McCaferty again. "Why don't you go home? Can't you see you're not wanted?" McCaferty looked down sadly at his half-empty beer bottle. E.L. said nothing, tired of talk.

"My child, I have no home to go to," McCaferty said. He looked at her. There was no pity in her stare. "I sold my loving wife for a train ticket years ago and packed up my three children to hock along the way. And now I'm wealthy but I don't have a place to spend my money and nobody to spend it with, except you two carefree young people."

"Bullshit," Vera said, but McCaferty could tell he had interested her because she did not look away.

"Yes, when I was only 21 I decided the life on the farm was not the life for me. My wife was always telling me that I thought more of drink than I did of her, until finally she convinced me and I sold her for 50 dollars to a dealer in white slaves. This was a long time ago, when 50 dollars was a lot of money." He paused for effect with a faraway expression on his face. Vera said, "Bullshit," again, but with less disdain than before, as if she might want him to continue.

"And my three charming little girls and my trunk and I rode the train to San Francisco, city of the Golden Gate, where the Chinee women live. There I changed my way of living, gave up the habits of a decent husband, father and provider, and I devoted my waking hours to hellraising." He leaned forward to fix them with a steady, bland pause. They were looking at him. "And it was not long before I had drunk up nearly all my 50 dollars and I had to ask my three charming daughters which wanted to be the first to go. A difficult decision to make, but Elsie volunteered, adventuress that she was, and I sold her to a German ship captain for 300 marks — what was then something like 100 dollars. Twice as much as I had got for my lovely wife. But that's the way it is out at the West Coast."

"I was out there once," Vera said slowly, as if testing him with a lie.

"Then you know jus what I mean. Well, 100 dollars and one daughter less to buy milk for, I was again ready for the Chinee women and Puerto Rican rum. I was livin high on the hog. Every night I'd go to a different fancy night club, buy drinks around for everyone in the place and those passing by on the sidewalk out front. In those days they had wooden sidewalks. And naturally at that rate the 100 dollars from dear Elsie lasted me only two months and then I was down and out again, the scorn of all those for whom I'd boughten Puerto Rican rum. All good-time Charlies. Know what I mean?"

E.L. nodded his head solemnly.

"But I looked at it this way — I owed it to them." Vera and E.L. continued to look at him. "They were jus poor people who never had a good time, too stingy to buy their own drinks, so it was up to some good Samaritan soul to provide for them. And I was the good Samaritan. So another daughter had to go. This time it was the youngest, Eustacia. She was a pretty little girl of three years with golden hair and a smile that sent the clouds into fits of laughter. But I knew — don't cry," he said quickly to Vera who hung her head from too much drink, " — but I knew that I could never provide the kind of life she deserved, since I was something of a carefree, ne'er-do-well sort of person, and I knew that no matter what fate befell her, she would still have that same cherubic smile on her face, that same gleam of inner happiness in her eye. "Ah she was a dear." He leaned back to relish her memory. "So I sold her to a prince or a shah, I can't recall which, and the last I heard from her, many years ago, she was married to an Egyptian prince and was one of a harem of 600 wives, of all nationalities. The last word I heard from her was a letter of thanks. Well, I got the fantastic sum of 200 dollars for little Eustacia and it was the same old routine all over again, having to pay for the happiness of others while I sat and brooded, lonely, in a corner thinking of all the cheap whiskey and rum I had drunk and how much there was yet to drink. Ah, back then I was quite a man. In San Francisco there used to be the drinking marathons. Sometimes as many as 200 hard-drinking men would enter a contest, putting up something like 50 dollars just to get a chance to out-drink the other men and win the big prize money."

"And you won, I suppose," Vera said.

"I've never been the same since. I think it was that terrible two weeks of steady drinking that was the turning point of my life. Ever since that fateful event I've never completely regained my strength. Well, that drinking marathon lasted two weeks. The rules were you had to keep the pace of the fastest drinker and if someone drank a quart in an hour, everybody else had to drink a quart to keep in the running. The event was held in the huge Cow Palace out there. Millions of people from all over the world came to see the contest. Well as you could imagine with a rule like that the contenders thinned out pretty quick. After just three hours of drinking there were only 150 left. One of those who had fallen out, as it were, went to sleep and slept three weeks straight through before his wife discovered he wasn't asleep but dead. Already embalmed. After the first day the contenders were down to 25 in number. That night drinking stopped. We all had to sleep on army cots there in front of those millions of people. Some of the drinkers used medical treatments to keep them in shape for competition, raw eggs and sheep's milk, milkweed stew, black coffee and every other outlandish thing you could think of. But not me. And that's why I won. The others didn't drop out because of the whiskey so much as it was from the way they punished their stomachs with those home remedies. During that two weeks I ate nothing at night except spare ribs and brown gravy and drank nothing but sassafras tea."

"God," Vera said. E.L. listened sternly.

"Well the drinking the second day was slow until I took the lead and began to set a faster pace. Ten men dropped out after the first hour. That left jus 15 men, counting yours truly. But those I was drinkin against were truly drinkers. Not one of them said a foolish word. We sat around a huge table with the whiskey quarts out there in the middle with a bright spotlight on us with the eyes of all those who had paid two and three dollars a ticket for a seat, bringing box lunches and bedrolls to see the best drinkers of the world compete. I remember one of those final 14 was from Tibet. He said he'd learned to drink on a fermented stone water made from grinding up granite and adding milk so it'd ferment. He was the second best drinker, next to me.

"After the first week we were just five in number. The betting was hot

19

and heavy. I remember one of the Rockefellers was there and he bet I think it was 500,000 on the nose on me. It was all the cash he had at the time and the amount he won gave him the start that fine eastern family has built into a fortune. All that, built on my carefree younger days' impetuosity and eagerness for havin fun. The five of us were pretty grim about it. We'd stopped joking each other and spent our waking hours concentrating on the drinking, spending our sleeping hours dreaming about the most dreadful things, as you can imagine.

"After 11 days there was only that fellow from Tibet and me. We sat opposite each other and matched each other drink for drink. I remember he had a long, crooked nose and every time he took a drink it'd wrinkle up and vapor fumes issued from his nostrils, because by then the whiskey we were drinking was pretty cheap stuff, having drunk up nearly all the better brands the city could provide."

"And this is supposed to be the truth?" Vera asked.

"I have never lied about anything important in my life," McCaferty answered her. "Well this Tibetan and me were grim as death about it, wanting that 10,000 dollars prize money. Runner-ups got nothin — winner take all. I was still setting the pace, but I felt pretty sick, having run out of sassafras tea to settle my stomach at night. I figured the battle was at the point where I had to make a move to either wipe him out or wipe out myself, elsewise we were going to kill off each other, so I picked up this full quart bottle, and at that stage of the competition it was heavy as a ton, and I put it to my lips and with my eyes closed and seeing the angels flapping their wings descending to fetch me to my heavenly rest, I drained every last drop of the vile stuff. The Tibetan blinked his eyes at me, I was told later, because though I was standing and bowing to the thunderous applause I received from the ever-increasing audience, I couldn't think too clear and I don't remember much at all of my moment of triumph. Well the Tibetan picked up the nearest quart bottle and stood and commenced to drain his as well. Then he stared back at me with his nose twitching like a rabbit's.

"I thought for sure I'd met my match in this wild man from Tibet until he gave me this silly grin, like he'd just seen a gnat's pecker, and he keeled over. It took him a year to recover, and as I say I ain't felt the same since."

"And you won?" Vera said.

"I read about it later," McCaferty said.

"What'd you do with the prize money?" E.L. asked.

"Well before I could get my wits about me I was talked into giving it to charity. I broke my health and squandered my reward on charity. And there you got the sad story of my greatest adventure in life — ruined by a moment of weakness. Now I'm doomed to walk the earth telling my story to anybody who'll listen."

"It sure is a sad story," Vera said.

"The truth is always sad, my dear," McCaferty said, feeling for a moment as if he were about to cry.

They were silent a long time, studying the cluttered table before them.

"What happened to the other daughter?" Vera asked. "You said you had three and you sold two of them."

"The third one, Karanina, eloped with a one-armed cowboy and became the celebrated Child Bride of Galveston, Texas. I'm sure you've heard of her." They both nodded their heads slowly.

"Oh I could tell you things that'd make you shout with amazement," McCaferty said mournfully.

But the waitress was at their table again and drinks were ordered round again. E.L. asked McCaferty if he would like a drink of whiskey. "No, E.L., ever since that ordeal in San Francisco I've left off my hard liquor."

Vera was now almost friendly to him, softer, now that he had shared his suffering with her as she had bared her suffering to him while talking to E.L. McCaferty did not feel any remorse for making them listen to his story, for he was sure there were many parts of it true, somewhere.

There was another strip tease, but a different girl did this dance, an older woman who, although she was not as pretty as Vera, knew better how to use the fat of her body.

It was nearly two a.m. when E.L. said he was ready to go. He was drunk again, having borrowed some money from Vera, who was also quite drunk. McCaferty was pleasantly drunk. The tavern was beginning to empty.

"Why don't you come home with us?" Vera asked McCaferty. Coming from her, the offer surprised him.

"Yeah, Mack. You don't have any place to go, do you?" E.L. asked.

"I'd be in the way and you don't know me well enough to take me home ..."

"Aw go to hell," E.L. said loudly. "If we didn't want you to we wouldn ask you, would we, huh?"

"All right, don't get sore."

They decided to take E.L.'s car and put Vera's behind the tavern. Vera had on high-heels and nearly fell several times in the gravel of the parking lot. She walked between them and they all laughed and McCaferty felt in the same moment both young and older than he was.

They all three got in the front seat of the little Chevrolet. E.L. convinced them he had driven as many miles drunk as he had sober and could drive a car from the Frolic Club to Benton blindfolded. But they were silent on the drive to Benton, watching the road. E.L. concentrated hard on the apparently flat surface of the highway ahead. It seemed to be merely a motion picture on the windshield, it was as if they were not moving but watching a film on the windshield. The wind roaring in the open windows of the car, for they were driving fast, did not give them a feeling of movement — it gave McCaferty a remote lost feeling, as if he were at sea, or on a high cliff and the wind was a storm that did not blow against him but howled a mournful story that he overheard. It was grim, and because he was drunk he felt a premonition of something sinister coming; the wind always seemed to talk to him of his death.

E.L. regularly drove off onto to the shoulder of the road but managed each time to get the car back onto the pavement. It was a frightening trip for Vera, McCaferty could tell, for when E.L. would drive off the road she leaned back in the seat, her body stiff.

At last they reached Benton. The city square, around the two-story, limestone county courthouse, was deserted. The street lights gave the small town a ghostly, gray, wet look. This is Benton, he thought, and was for a moment very sober and tense. He wondered if E.L. and Vera felt the same animal pang he felt. Vera lit a cigaret and leaned back against the seat.

McCaferty said, "From the way you two have been talkin I think that house's crowded enough without me comin along too. Whyn't you jus let me out here somewhere and I'll ..."

"You shut up," E.L. said. McCaferty sensed that E.L. felt the same coldness; but what the "coldness" was McCaferty could not tell. He was drunk, he knew that, and that explained a great deal about his premonitions.

Vera said, "The house's real big and there's room for 15, 20 people."

"I still don't have any business."

"We need you to fix coffee." E.L. said.

The house was about three blocks from the city square. It was a large, old house, a wooden frame building, two-story, the kind the rich built 50 years ago in small midwestern towns. There were no lights in the windows of the house. E.L. parked the car in the street in front of the house and they got out and walked up the sidewalk to the porch.

E.L. said quietly, "My wife sleeps upstairs." pointing to a second-floor window, "in that room there. We got plenty room in the house."

"This's a pretty old house," McCaferty said.

"It's my wife's house," E.L. said.

There were a few metal lawn chairs on the long front porch and two wooden rocking chairs. The boards of the porch were old and soft and creaked as the three of them slowly and carefully crossed the porch. The only light on the porch came from a street lamp up the street. E.L.'s face was in the shadows of one of the posts on the porch; looking at E.L., McCaferty forgot what the young man looked like. "Let's go on in," Vera said. They went in quietly, E.L. stumbling against a table invisible in the dark, old-smelling room. The floor in the large living room creaked as did the floor of the long dining room. They walked single file, slowly, E.L. leading the way. In the kitchen E.L. turned on a light.

McCaferty was surprised. He did not know exactly what he had expected, but the squat, old stove in the corner of the kitchen, the gray tile sink with the cast-iron pump, the wooden ice box, the concrete floor, all this surprised him. He thought about the rest of the house and knew immediately the other dark rooms they had passed through were also like this.

E.L. pointed to the cook stove. "You know how to operate one of these things?"

"Yes," McCaferty said.

He got some wood out of the box beside the stove and started a fire. Vera put coffee in a pot of water and they sat down at the large square table in the center of the room to wait for the coffee. McCaferty looked at the tablecloth. The cloth was one tourists buy in a state or country they visit. This one had the minerals, resources, scenic sights, and pictures of famous people from the state of Illinois. There was a large bronze-brown picture of Lincoln in the corner of the cloth. McCaferty stared at the tablecloth while Vera and E.L. smoked cigarets and stared silently at the high ceiling.

"That means my wife's been to Illinois," E.L. said flatly.

McCaferty looked at the young man; E.L.'s face was expressionless. "She'll talk your arm off about Chicago. And she's great on Effingham. Don't ask her about Cairo, it'll embarrass her. She's never been there."

"Adaline's a little," Vera tapped the side of her head with her finger and McCaferty nodded slowly, though he didn't understand.

"She fell down once when she was a little girl and she never been the same since," E.L. said grimly, then looked into McCaferty's eyes and smiled sheepishly. "She fell out of a barn loft I think. Right on her head."

"That's too bad," McCaferty said.

"No it ain't," E.L. said. "She likes it this way. She's happy. You stay around tomorrow and you'll see her and you'll see what I mean. She's happy as hell. Have her tell you bout Jimmy Rogers. She knew him back when he was singin on the radio, long time ago."

"She'd be okay if she wasn't so goddamn crazy," Vera said.

"No she wouldn." E.L. leaned forward, putting his elbows on the table, philosophically wrinkling his brow and squinting his eyes. "If she had all her marbles nobody could stand her. She's better off this way. And she's happy, too."

"She this way when you married her?"

E.L. nodded his head slowly, not looking at McCaferty. "I thought I could maybe help her. But it jus didn work out, Mack."

They were quiet again, thinking about E.L.'s wife, Adaline. Soon the coffee boiled and Vera got up from the table to get cups.

E.L. leaned his head forward. "What really caused it was she was married once before and had a little girl that got killed and she jus never got over it. That was a long time ago and she jus never got over it."

McCaferty mumbled, "The loss of one's children is indeed tragic," too low for E.L. to hear. His mind was beginning to clear and he remembered what E.L. had said, and it did not seem quite natural to him that E.L.

would marry the woman to see if he could "help" her. But he remembered that E.L. was still drunk. The young man now sat slumped back in his chair, his chin down on his chest, his red-rimmed eyes staring bleakly at the map of Illinois on the tablecloth. Vera poured the coffee and sat down and the three of them sat watching the cups steaming. The oppression of fatigue and the silently crackling, slow fire of consuming time made them silent. McCaferty rolled himself a cigaret. They could hear nothing but the occasional popping of the fire inside the cookstove. Now and then a board in the floor or one of the walls would pop, restless in an inanimate way from the endless immobility of the old house. The old place reminded McCaferty that he was 68.

They sat drinking coffee for an hour, until about four o'clock. E.L. did most of the talking, which was not much. McCaferty did not say five words. Then Vera cleared off the table and said it was time to go to bed. She and E.L. decided to be very quiet and sleep in the second bedroom on the second floor that was at the far end of the house from where E.L.'s wife slept. McCaferty was to sleep on the sofa in the living room.

They all made final trips to the toilet on the screened-in back porch and then turned out the light in the kitchen. Dawn was growing. It did not seem to McCaferty that only one day had passed since he stood on the bank of the Wabash River and watched dawn change the color of the water from black to gray.

"What about when your wife wakes up?" McCaferty asked E.L.

"We'll lock the door of our room. She won't bother you. She'll think you're some important oil man."

"I don't look very important."

"She thinks everbody that comes here's important."

Then Vera and E.L. went upstairs to the bedroom and he heard them walking slowly on the creaking floor. He went into the living room and sat down on the sofa. The room was gray with a weak eerie light that did not seem to come in the white-lace curtained windows, but seemed to either rise from the thin rug on the floor, or emanate from the yellow papered walls. The room and this time of night were depressing, and the burden of McCaferty's life was his sensitivity and susceptibility to depression.

McCaferty thought about E.L. and Vera. He would sleep a while in the living room, get up when E.L.'s wife came down, talk to her a while, maybe get something to eat for breakfast, and then leave. He would go back to Spring Garden, but he had plenty of time and there was no need to worry about when he would leave. That was one of the advantages of being on the bum.

He looked at one of the pictures hanging on the walls of the room. The frames of the pictures were dark, thick, baroquely carved, the kind popular at the turn of the century.

The picture he looked at showed a lake at either sundown or sunup surrounded by mountains; as day approached and the room became better lighted the old man could see the details of the picture. He distinguished a large stag at one side of the lake, at one side of the picture, and at the other side of the picture, at the other side of the lake, was an Indian in a canoe. The stag and the Indian were looking at each other.

McCaferty slipped his feet out of his shoes and lay down on the hard, faded-gray sofa and closed his eyes. He was very tired. He was glad he had drunk beer instead of whiskey.

THINGS IN PLACE

THE DUST CLOUD FOLLOWED THE ARROYO down to the valley and turned when it reached the highway, as Haskel knew it would, fanning wide on both sides of the road and coming straight toward him.

Haskel pulled the truck off the road, cut the motor, and rolling down the window leaned out. He heard far off a buzzing roar like a storm of hornets. He took out his teeth and put them in the breast pocket of his denim jacket. Then rolled up the window and drove on slowly, half-off the road to give them plenty of room.

Still over a mile away he could make them out, thirty or forty abreast so they wouldn't get their own dust. At this distance they were giant insects.

For three days and nights they had been out here, and Haskel had watched them. (Now for the first time they saw him — the flanks of the wide line drew in and they came even faster.) He had watched with binoculars and concluded that above all they were constantly in motion, even at night in their camp, jumping on their motorcycles and riding off as if they all had been stung by the same dire impulse.

Or they danced all night, and he saw fights in the yellow light, and they rode around and around the bonfire, though in the distance it appeared they rode into the bonfire and became the fire itself—out of existence on a dare and back again. In the light of day they plunged headlong, whether down the highway, along a trail, or straight across the desert — they didn't need roads. They shot off hills, cutting through the air forward-leaning and furious, as if enraged with the passivity of space.

Five hundred feet ahead of Haskel they slowed. Now they would block the road. There were even more than he thought — fifty, sixty. Women rode double behind some of them, lean long-legged women in jeans and leather, their faces shrewd as chromium, their eyes rapacious but at the same time paradoxically indifferent — as though their minds were elsewhere, or they were in fact elsewhere and these were their souls, fled to the desert. The men were big, long-armed, etched with tattoos. Grinning, their mouths were slashed with the obscene eagerness of wolves. Astraddle their bikes, revving the motors, they tightened a gauntlet down the middle of the road, and as Haskel entered they leaned on the truck and pounded the fenders, grinning in at him.

Then he was through them. In the mirror watched them spread out again in a line. When they were at least two miles down the road Haskel put his teeth back in. He slowed at the arroyo road. Up there was their camp. After glancing in the mirror, Haskel drove by. If he went up there, they might see his dust and come back.

He went down the highway to the dirt road that led to his place. And nothing beyond but the canyon rim and, over it, the first of two buttes staring at each other across forty miles. He called them the Big Ideas. Because they looked sure of why they were here.

The truck bounced, tilted on the road, slowly climbing the canyon wall. Then he saw the cabin. A window, crooked chimney, a shed out back. Beyond a narrow meadow, cut with a stream, a forest spread to the rim.

Haskel got out and held his breath, listening. Heard in the woods the crash of hard running. Then the dog, gray-brown, quick and wolflike except it didn't have the absolute, improbable bigness of a wolf, came out of the woods and into the meadow. Haskel squared off to meet it and it lunged against him and banged its jaws in his face, just short of his nose. He choked it, it chewed his shoulder, they stagger-waltzed a big circle and crashed against the truck. Haskel sat on the running board, panting, and the dog stood in front of him, panting too, tongue out, eyes laughing. 'The motorcycle people," Haskel announced. The dog shut its mouth, ears pricked. "All of them. We had a parley-vous."

Haskel unloaded the supplies from the cab of the truck and went to the shed to chop wood. The dog wandered off but came back when it saw Haskel walking from the stream toward the cabin with the bucket. They went in and ate.

Later they went out front, watched the valley go down in purple. The sky became night. Abruptly the lights of Lordsburg thirty miles away winked into being.

In the middle of the night the cabin moved. He sat up. The dog, sleeping on the floor beside the bed, stood and yawned in the dark. Haskel went to the door.

Wind — huge and preoccupied, moved down the canyon, shaking loose, changing.

Haskel got the binoculars, moved them slowly up the arroyo, looking for the yellow light of the bonfire.

"They're gone," he said. The dog wagged its tail.

He built a fire and put on coffee. The dog curled down and went to sleep.

When the coffee was ready Haskel cooked breakfast. "They're gone for good," he whispered. He ate some and put the rest down for the dog when it woke.

Motor and headlights off, down the long hill the truck rolled, silent except for the creaking of springs and the skee of brakes. Haskel stopped short of the highway, staring at the dim corona above Lordsburg. He turned on the radio and found what he liked — cat music, he called it, coarse and jangling, from Mexico and fading off in miles, laced with static, then coming back louder than before.

An immense breath, change moved over the valley. First light.

He switched off the radio, started the motor, and pulled onto the highway.

He reached the arroyo road as gray dawn opened the sky. The hills were purple-black.

He walked around the bowl where they had camped. The wind had scavenged footprints and tire tracks, and everything else it could take. Left behind a ripped-out beercase wedged between two bushes. And some cans scattered here and there, half-buried. Haskel kicked through the remains of the bonfire — the charred carcass of some huge beast they had cooked whole and ate on the ground. He moved farther out, circled the camp. Snagged in a bush he found a silk scarf, black and green. He sniffed it but already the desert had taken the smell of the person.

Instead of returning down the arroyo he drove out a trail they had cut with their motorcycles. It forked then crossed other trails. He turned onto one. And it crossed other trails. These were their streets, a city with no houses or people. He swung a turn, topping a dune, the nose of the truck in the sky, and when it dipped Haskel slammed on the brakes.

They turned. The big one had a huge sharp chin, making him devilish, self-sure. He stared at Haskel, seemed to already start telling him what to do. The little one got up and helped him to his feet — and the little one was a woman, a girl, her hair hiding her face and partially covering her breasts. The man put his arm over her shoulders, leaned on her, and they came around to the side of the truck. Haskel rolled down his window.

She pushed her hair back with one hand. Her face was small and round. After looking at each other for a moment, she and Haskel spoke at the same time: "What are you doing out here?" — and she said, "Take us."

"To Lordsburg?" he said.

The man lifted his head, his eyes bright black. "No."

"No," the girl said to Haskel, her lips straight, smug.

"We got to stay awake," the man said and swayed back on his heels.

"Away," the girl said, grabbing him with both arms. "Away."

"You're staying out here?" Haskel said.

The girl stepped up on the running board. Leaning in, her face nearly touching Haskel's, she whispered, her eyes gleaming with excitement: "Take Hopalong and me to your place."

"My place?" He nodded. "Okay. Get in."

She went around the truck with Hopalong and opened the door. She stood behind him and pushed to get him up into the truck — and before he was even inside, sprawled knees wide apart, Haskel smelled blood and saw Hopalong's pants were soaked. The girl jumped in after him and slammed the door. "I'm Lily."

Haskel nodded and started the truck. Hopalong's head thunked against the rear window. Lily stared across him at Haskel, her face gray and without expression, her eyes like paraffin.

They helped Hopalong into the cabin and he shoved them away. He sat down at the table and grabbed up the cards with which Haskel played solitaire. His big fingers fumbled with the piece of string tied around the deck, then he shuffled the cards. Grinning fiercely, his bulging cheeks knotting his eyes, he rapped the cards on the table. "Stud," he said slyly and winked at Haskel.

"Come on," Lily said, tugging at his arm. She took the cards from him and pulled harder — "Over here. Come on, Hopalong." He got up and when he looked away from Haskel his mouth fell open, as if discovering the cabin was vast, infinite, with long corridors of light: far away, tiny in the distance, he saw a bed.

He collapsed across it. Haskel was building a fire when he heard a splop and turned to see the bloody trousers in the middle of the floor. With a piece of kindling he carried them out to the shed. When he returned, Hopalong, covered with blankets, lay turned to the wall. Lily wore one of Haskel's shirts, the sleeves rolled up. She was frying bacon and when it was done she took it to Hopalong and whispered too low for Haskel to hear.

"Hopalong won't eat." Haskel looked up. She stood beside him, her hands on her hips. "He used to eat all the time — you know? He was almost famous, he ate so much. Now, nothing. What'll I do?"

Haskel nodded. "You came to the right man: I don't know."

He went outside. The wind was up, rushing down the canyon like a big reckless boy. Haskel ducked around the corner. The sky scooped deep into the valley, a storm moving in. There would be snow, a great wall of snow.

The dog sailed around the corner on a gust of wind. "She kick you out?" Haskel yelled and grabbed its tail. The dog snarled, jerked its head around and snapped at him. When he let go it lunged away and barked. Haskel barked back, and the dog liked that, its eyes gleeful.

The food she cooked for Hopalong was on the table. Haskel sat down and ate it.

Then he built up the fire and got his pipe. He pulled up his chair and almost immediately was lost in the flames' invention. He returned only when, floating up from canyons, he put on another log.

The dog lifted its head, ears pricked. Slowly Haskel turned.

Lily wore only the shirt now, the shirt tail reaching halfway down her thighs. She tiptoed across the room and leaned down to him. Then her face went blank, her eyes faded as if she had forgotten everything.

Hopalong is dead, Haskel thought. That was it. He didn't need to ask her.

"I'll sleep here," Lily whispered.

He heard her making a pallet on the floor behind him. Then she was still, there was nothing but the fire and the wind above the cabin. When he woke, the fire was down and the wind had lain. The sky had the dense silence of snow.

He looked over his shoulder; she lay in a ball under the blankets, her head covered. On the edge of the pallet the dog also lay in a ball, its eyes open, staring at Haskel.

Morning. Haskel went out into a gray lull. A great drift buried half the cabin. Below, through thick air, the valley was shallowed with snow and seemed so close Haskel could have climbed to his roof and jumped clear across it. The woods had moved nearer during the storm, the trees immense and dour, shadows deep as caves hunkering under the branches sagging with the weight of the snow.

Haskel tromped out to the shed and got the ax, logs. Scooped off the block and a place to stand, and swung the ax. The log split with a sharp crack that shot down the hill, and Haskel looked up. Air quivered around the cabin. The door slowly opened.

Roaring, Hopalong ran out naked into the snow, his back and shoulders brownish yellow, waxen. The roar hung in the air. He ran hard, then stopped, bent forward, coughing.

Haskel ran down to the cabin, then onto Hopalong's trail. He caught up just short of the woods. "Hold it." Haskel panted. Louder — "Hold it!"

Hopalong swung around, reared, rising and opening his arms like a bear turning on dogs, and Haskel saw the huge wide chest, the stomach black with hair wedging down to the bush at the base of the stomach, as if pointing to what Haskel didn't see. For there was not the big thrusting cock Haskel expected. Instead, a gash grinned blood over a white sprig of tendon. Running pumped fresh blood over what had dried on Hopalong's thighs, ringing the snow red around his knees.

Haskel looked up to the man's face and could tell by Hopalong's eyes that he didn't know if Haskel had seen or not, that Hopalong no longer knew. Had somehow forgotten what there was about him that another man would find amazing. Hopalong's eyes, large and baffled, hardly paused on Haskel, as if Haskel were just one of a crowd floating before him in the gray light.

"Let's go back," Haskel said.

"Huh?" — and his eyes found Haskel.

"Back to my place. Come on."

Slowly shaking his head, Hopalong made the noise again, the roar that was almost a word but just outside meaning, louder and louder, and he clenched his fists and drew them up. Haskel backed but not fast enough, Hopalong was on him like a falling tree.

Numb deep in snow. Not thinking now. For minutes, maybe longer. Haskel was far away from himself, though now he saw his hands, red with cold. His hands were pushing at the yellow sack of flesh that was the naked man, and with strange easiness Haskel pushed him away.

Haskel sat up, breathing hard and looked at the sky. His face was blunt numb, maybe he no longer had a face, accepted the possibility that he didn't: Hopalong had lost his cock and was going around taking faces.

Thirty feet away Hopalong and Lily sat side by side in the snow, their backs to Haskel. They were talking low but in the silence Haskel heard them distinctly. "To Phoenix," she said.

"No. Nothing," Hopalong said.

"Bubba's there. And Nadine."

"Is that Bubba?" Hopalong said and looked over his shoulder at Haskel.

"No," Lily said. "That's just him. We can sleep in his house."

Hopalong got to his feet and moved away slowly, Lily calling to him. Haskel rose and started after him, running easily, the snow carrying him on waves.

Hopalong entered the first line of trees and disappeared. Then Haskel saw him again, slipping in and out of view, gliding deeper into the woods. Haskel followed, running hard, but looking over his shoulder he saw the cabin below, a straight line of woodsmoke rising from the chimney.

Ahead, Haskel saw Hopalong down a straight corridor through the woods. Going downhill now, they flew through luminous blue-green silence.

It would be a matter of minutes, an hour or two at most. The fire crackled excitedly, the flames danced.

"We can go to Albuquerque," Lily whispered. Hopalong lay flat on his back. Lily leaned down, her hands on his chest, her lips to his ear. Hopalong's eyes were closed and he breathed heavily, his lips flubbering. Then he was silent. Lily stopped whispering. Haskel turned. She sat on the side of the bed, her legs crossed and her hands in her lap, watching Haskel with the corners of her mouth tucked up primly.

They dragged Hopalong out to the truck; nothing could get him there. Hopalong sat stiffly at the steering wheel, ready to go. Haskel slammed the truck door and he and Lily went into the cabin.

Lily sat at the table and picked up the deck of cards and shuffled them. Haskel rolled her a cigarette and one for himself. "Thanks," she said and dealt.

"My mom says, 'Lily, someday you'll get into something you can't get out of.' I tell her, 'Moms, don't lose any sleep worrying about me.' But maybe she's right.

"Some people just don't care — you know? Bubba don't care. He don't give a shit for anything. When Nadine got busted in Cruces she called Bubba and Bubba said, 'Tough shit.'" She was silent as they played the hand. She won.

She took the papers and tobacco and rolled another cigarette. Then she shuffled and dealt again. "Mom says, 'Lily, you're crazy.' She says that because of what happened to Frieda. Frieda's my sister. Not my little sister, her name's Nadine. But Frieda's my big sister that got killed in a crash on Looper Lane in Phoenix. And Mom won't let me forget, like it was my fault. So I tell her if I'm crazy it's because she drove me crazy talking about Frieda. That's what Bubba tells me. Me and Bubba were doing Cunt City when I met Hopalong."

She ground out her cigarette and stood. She pulled the shirt up and over her head as if it were a sweater. With both hands she smoothed back her long hair, her breasts rising and slowly lowering. She came around the table and stepped between Haskel's knees. Putting an arm around his neck, she cupped a breast and put the nipple to his lips. "When Frieda got it she was riding back of Bubba. Bubba swerved to miss a Jag and went up the back of a Mercury and jumped a Pontiac Le Mans and a Chevy van before they came down. Frieda never knew what hit her, but she died with a smile on her face."

Lily took off her trousers and lay naked on the bed. She crossed her legs, resting her ankle on the raised knee of her other leg.

"Frankly, I can take it or leave it. Not like Nadine, who has to have it at least every ten hours and if she don't she gets nauseous. But Frieda was just the opposite. Doing it gave her gas, so she quit. She hadn't done it for six days when she racked up on Looper Lane.

"You got a nice one. You should've seen Hopalong's. It really was what you'd call remarkable. That was why the Motor Maniacs cut it off. Bunch of jealous little pricks — that's what I told Hopalong. But it didn't console him enough."

As Haskel lay down, Lily jumped up. She ran across the room, turned, her arms spread wide against the wall behind her. "Ready?" She squatted like a frog, her knees wide apart, and leaped. She sailed through the air and landed on Haskel.

Her hair hung down, framing their faces. She smiled brightly. "There! Gottum Daddy's whanger."

Lily got out, slammed the door, and stood beside the road. Haskel scooted down, it would be a long wait. But then he heard on the silence a flat gray hum. He looked. A dot wavered on the horizon. Then gradually louder, the sound of a motor, tires on concrete. The dot became a car, its windshield glinting. It came fast though by now the driver could see Lily beside the road, thumb out, her other hand on her hip.

The motor cut, there was the strain of brakes and tires, and the car stopped beside Lily. The man at the wheel sat looking straight ahead as Lily got in. The car accelerated, and Lily looked out, but not at Haskel. Her face behind the window disappeared as the car smoothly sped off, two, three miles away, shrinking to a gray speck.

Haskel drove the truck onto the highway and headed the opposite direction, toward Lordsburg. He hadn't gone far when a caravan of cars pulling horse trailers passed him. When he came to town more cars and trailers were parked along the street.

He parked the truck on a side street. When he walked back, on the main street twenty or thirty women wearing white ten-gallon hats and white leather jackets and pants with long fringe, were riding palominos. The women smiled and waved at the people. They rode two blocks down the street, turned, and rode back.

Haskel bought supplies, then headed back out, driving slowly down the straight highway, looking off across the plain widening with afternoon shadows. He and the dog went to the shed to see how Hopalong was doing. He sat waiting in the corner. In a day or two when the snow was off Haskel would put him in the meadow.

Haskel went into the house and ate supper. He sat at the table a while, then moved across to the bed and was asleep before sundown.

He woke to the wind, or maybe it was a coyote. But again he heard the dull snow-muffled clomp. He went to the window.

They came single file, a long procession, more than he had seen in town, all in white leather with fringe and big white hats, all riding palominos shining in the night.

He backed away and stood in the middle of the room with his hands lifted. Then turned, grabbed up a log and threw it on the fire. As he heard the shudder-snort of the horses just outside the door he reached for the coffee pot. He had just banged it on the grate when the door opened wide and he turned to see the first of them leaning forward to clear the doorway as she rode into the cabin. The horse's eyes were huge, dazzled by the light.

MRS. BELL AND HER DOG

THE DOG STOOD CHAINED AT THE CORNER of the house. It looked back toward the alley, where Tyler peeked around the corner of the garage, but it didn't see him. It stood there — big, black, slick, its eyes intense. It turned and, dragging its heavy chain between its feet, went around the side of the house. Tyler waited. He knew all the dog's tricks. He waited for it to pop its head around the corner. But it didn't this time.

Tyler took a deep breath and stepped from behind the garage to the fence. With both hands he carefully opened the gate. He pushed it open slowly, then shut it after him, but he didn't hook it — in case the dog would suddenly come around the corner. The dog's chain was connected to an iron ring in the foundation of the house. It was long enough to allow the dog to reach the back porch.

Tyler hesitated a moment and then hurried across the yard to the porch. He reached the old wooden steps and he labored up them, holding onto the wobbly handrail, and then he was to the screen door of the porch and inside.

He paused, catching his breath, hoping for a moment that the dog would come around the corner and see that he had made it again, and he even thought of calling it — it didn't have a name, just "Yoo hoo," as Mrs. Bell called it, but that was what she called everyone. But he didn't want to taunt the dog. If he called it, it would come lunging around the corner, its great mouth open, its eyes furious, and it would see him standing up there on the porch inside the screen door. And then it would know he would be coming out again eventually, and Tyler knew the dog was capable of remembering, and he also knew it was willing to spend an entire day just waiting for him.

He crossed the sagging wooden floor of the porch and pushed open the door of the kitchen. He smelled the house's odors of kraut, dust, and old woman. He went in. The sink and cabinet were cleared, which meant Mrs. Bell was now in the front part of the big dark house. Or it meant — and this was even better — that she was next door at the two old sisters who also rented out a room or two. The old women gossiped and complained about the men they rented to — Tyler had heard them one afternoon when the sisters were visiting Mrs. Bell.

Tyler slowly and carefully crossed the linoleum floor and went into the hallway. Out of the kitchen, the house was cold. Dust was thick in the gray hall carpet.

He listened. He heard nothing — cold, deep silence. Which meant, he hoped and was almost certain, that Mrs. Bell was next door, for if she was taking a nap, as she sometimes did in the middle of the morning, he would hear her powerful snoring. There was a chance, though, that she was still in the house — that she had seen him come in and was waiting for him to try slipping upstairs to his room, and when he was to his room she would come up behind him and yell so loud it would almost knock him down, "Well! What have we here!" and she would grin, all the intense, discordant features of her face exaggerated as she tried to open wider her small gray eyes. She always talked to him as though he were a child — he was certain she thought she could get away with it because she was old. He knew the type from other landladies over the years. They got away with a lot of things because they were old.

She hated the big dog. The tenant who had the room Tyler now occupied had given Mrs. Bell the dog as payment for three months' back rent. The man had won the dog in a card game and told her it was well worth the seventy-five dollars he owed her. Mrs. Bell kept the dog because she couldn't find anyone who would give her seventy-five dollars for it. Also, there had been a burglary three houses down, and Mrs. Bell had a terrible fear of burglars. She kept two loaded guns in her bedroom, she told Tyler soon after he moved in, perhaps as a warning to him.

She also hated the dog because it ate so much. With strange pride she told him the dog ate so much she had to buy day-old bread.

"Bet you never heard of a dog that ate bread, did you?" she said, her mouth crooked in a grin.

"No," he said.

"Well if you wanta see somethin' pretty peculiar, just bring yourself out here a minute."

He followed her to the kitchen. She went over to the big wooden cupboard under the counter and got out a big loaf of bread. "Day-old," she said and rapped it on the counter edge. It was hard. "Then I keep it a week or two. See? He likes it hard. Gives his teeth somethin' to do."

Then she got a big knife from a drawer and cut off the end of the loaf. "This is the good part," she said and went to the old icebox in the corner. She got out a package of wieners, took one and held it up for Tyler to see, and put the rest back. "This is what he likes," she said and walked slowly, heavily over to the counter and the loaf again. She picked up the big knife and after glancing at Tyler, her small eyes expressionless, she stabbed into the end of the loaf again and again. She panted when she was finished making the hole. Then she stuck the wiener in the hole. She waddled over to another drawer and got a slice of bread. "I gotta keep some fresh for this part of it," and she wadded up the slice of bread and stopped up the end of the loaf behind the wiener.

"Now comes the good part," she said, and it looked like she winked at him.

She went to the back door. "Yoo hoo," she called and made a sucking tch tch. The dog came charging around the corner of the house, and Tyler held his breath. It leaped up the porch steps and reared on its hind legs against the screen door, and it was almost as tall as Mrs. Bell. Tyler knew the dog had seen him. He caught that moment when the dog's eyes were on him, a surprised moment, as if in its intense, hating mind flashed "Him Him," but then the dog saw the loaf as it stood reared up, its gaunt underside stretched before them — its sharp jutting ribs and the menacing thrust of its sex — the dog whined urgently and looked up from the loaf at Mrs. Bell and Tyler on the porch, and then Tyler realized Mrs. Bell was tee-heeing.

"D'you see that?" she said, turning and looking down at Tyler. "He smells the wiener inside it." Tyler nodded and looked away from her and at the dog again. There was an awful beauty in the dog — a valueless beauty, amazing, based on its intensity, its brutal thoughtlessness, its great size.

Then Mrs. Bell shoved against the screen door with her shoulder. When the door opened, it pushed the dog backwards off the top step and it fell, a furious scrape and clatter of claws and stiff, long legs. But even as it fell, it kept its long-snouted, sharp head erect on its neck and didn't take its eyes from the loaf as it fell down the stairs.

She reached out the screen door and tossed the loaf into the air.

The dog, already to its feet again, jumped into the air and caught the loaf in its mouth with a loud pow as the teeth crushed into the loaf, and it dropped to the ground and stood, feet apart, its eyes staring ahead without seeing, as it choked down the loaf in three bites, with head tilted back, its throat bulging as it swallowed. It sniffed the ground for the crumbs and then looked up at Mrs. Bell and Tyler on the porch.

"Now that's somethin', ain't it?" Mrs. Bell said. Tyler nodded and turned away from the door.

And maybe Mrs. Bell hated Tyler. And maybe that was to be expected. She said the usual cruel things — Did he get in for half-fare at the movies? Did he have a girlfriend? — and all the time she was asking him she would stare down at him with those small dark eyes, like cinders thumbed down into wet earth. But Tyler had learned long before Mrs. Bell to seem not to be getting the point of things said by landladies, clerks in stores, and kids on the street. But with the dog, she played two things she hated against each other.

She could chain it to the front door of the house. Or she could shorten the chain so the dog couldn't come clear to the back porch steps. Tyler had complained. When he did she said, "Well now. I reckon you can use the front door just as good as you can use the back, can't you?" There was that glint deep in her eye: she knew he couldn't manage the front steps. That first day she had stood on the porch and watched him as he tried to walk up the steep steps alone. He had finally to go up the steps one at a time, putting his suitcase two steps ahead of him and using both hands to hoist himself up onto each step. After he had got to the top, she told him he could try the steps on the back porch the next time, they might not be so bad.

But she wouldn't move the dog. She told him it wouldn't do any good to have a watchdog if it couldn't get to the door. "That's where the burglars will come in. The back door is the one you got to watch out for. You don't think they're going to come in the front way, do you?"

There were other things she did, too. When he first came to look at the room (that was before she got the dog), he noticed, first thing, that there

40

was a key in the door of the room. He was glad of that. (The reason he had been looking for a new place to live was he had trouble with his other landlady. She kept coming into his room.) But then after he moved to the room at Mrs. Bell's he discovered that the key had disappeared. He asked her about it. She squinted and said, "Why, no sir. There's no locked doors in this house, believe you me. I just won't have none of that here. Everything's got to be on the up and up around here. That's just the way it's gonna be." And she knew he couldn't right then and there move out, for she had (by mistake, she said, the hint of a grin moving beneath the flesh caked on her face) opened a letter that came for him at the new address. Tyler had very efficiently changed his address well in advance of moving, and then the letter came to Mrs. Bell's before he had even moved in.

It was from his sister. She said she was sorry she couldn't send more money so he could have his furniture moved. And there was a check enclosed for his next month's rent, plus fifteen dollars for him to live on.

And another thing, on the first day of the month Mrs. Bell came into his room at six o'clock and told him she wanted her rent money. After the first time she did it, Tyler tried to pay her on the day before, but she wouldn't take it. "No siree," she said loudly. "The first is on the first. If you give it to me sooner than that, it's an extra day on the other end, and that gets it all out of kilter. You got to remember, my friend, that I been rentin' out that room for twenty years. I know just exactly how to run my business, believe you me." And she did, too, for it was the next day that a bill collector tracked down for her the previous tenant and she got the dog for the back rent.

She came into his room just whenever she wanted to. To bring up a letter from his sister (the only mail he ever got). To see the windows were down when it was raining — like she thought he would sit and watch rain blow into his room.

He tried to push the big dresser over in front of the door, but it was too heavy even with the drawers out. There was a big overstuffed chair in the room, the bed, and the only piece of furniture he had been able to carry by himself from his other room — a small rocking chair.

There was no way he could keep her out of the room. And he couldn't confront her about it again. She would just stand there and bellow down at him, glee in her eyes and that little flesh-buried grin.

So he took it. There was nothing else to do.

He wrote letters to his sister and told her about Mrs. Bell, but he never sent them. He thought once of writing his sister a letter and going out and leaving it on the dresser where Mrs. Bell would see it when she went prowling around in his room. But it wouldn't do any good. When he came back, Mrs. Bell would catch him on the stairs and yell at him again about how all the doors in this house had to be unlocked at all times.

He had got a box at the post office and that stopped her from reading the letters his sister sent him. It cost him a lot of money to get the box just for the two letters a month from his sister — his check, sometimes with a short letter, and the longer, monthly letter, a page and a half in which his sister always said the same things about her husband, who was a paper hanger, and her two kids in high school. But the cost of the mailbox was worth it, and going to the post office gave him something to do.

That was where he had been today, and it was a good day, because he had got a letter from his sister.

He listened, and still heard no sound in the big house. He started upstairs, panting for breath after the first three steps. The rest of the way up to the second floor was an endless climb, and he started coughing from the dust he stirred up. He gritted his teeth and closed his eyes and climbed the stairs, knowing how far he had got without having to count the steps. When he was halfway up he stopped again, straightened up to hold onto the rail, and he was dizzy for a few moments. He turned around, for usually it was when he had got halfway up that Mrs. Bell appeared either at the head of the stairs — looming like a building — or yelled up from the foot of the stairs, for it was his coughing and gasping that let Mrs. Bell know he was going upstairs.

But apparently today she was next door. He sat down on the next step and rested, and then knowing she was out of the house gave him the strength to make it the rest of the way to the top.

He hurried down the hall past the door of an empty room, the bedroom, the enormous dark door of her room, then down to the end of the hall to his room. He went in and shut the door after himself. He looked to see if the key had reappeared in the lock. It hadn't.

He took off his jacket, sweater, and hat and put them up on the dresser.

He got the letter from his jacket pocket and moved the rocking chair closer to the window. He sat down.

He looked at the postmark — Sheboygan, September 3, PM He looked at his sister's handwriting, the smooth, graceful way she wrote his name: "Mr. Larry Tyler."

He slowly tore open the envelope and slid out the two sheets of stationery. A page and a half. He looked at the second sheet to see that his sister's husband hadn't added a P.S. at the end. Once a long time ago his sister's husband had added a note to her letter. In it he said he didn't mind at all sending money to Tyler because he knew Tyler would do the same for him. Tyler hadn't liked the P.S. The intentions were good, but he knew his sister had made him write it.

But this one didn't have a P.S. He started the chair rocking back and forth and he read the first page.

Dear Larry

How are you? Things here are fine I guess. Well as could be expected, ha ha! The kids are doing fine and we are all in good health. I hope you are in good health also, do take care of yourself.

Do you need a new overcoat for this winter? Let me know that. Also be sure and get some more galoshes if you need them because this winter will be a bad one I have a feeling!

He paused before he went on to the second page. He had decided a long time ago he would never again buy clothes in stores. He would get a catalogue, mail in the orders, and have the things sent to his box at the post office. That would be better. He read the second page of the letter.

Your room sounds real nice, you are lucky to find such a nice room so close to the post office and grocery store! I sometimes wish we lived closer to Sheboygan, but its nice for the kids here.

Let me hear from you. See you soon!

Sis

He read the letter again and then sat staring at it, not thinking except when in his mind he saw his sister's face, her lips moving, and he saw her laughing, silently as though he were looking at her through thick glass.

He folded the letter, put it back into its envelope, and folding it again, put it in his hip pocket. He got up from the rocking chair and went over to the overstuffed chair which he had scooted, his first day in the room, across from the bed with its back to the window. He took his shoes off and climbed up into the chair. He stood in the seat, leaning against the back, and stared out the window.

The view from this room was better than the one at the other room, but he didn't like it as much. He had told his sister he could see lots of trees and a street corner. The fact was, he could see more than that. He hadn't said that he could see the fronts of three houses, the entrance to an alley, and halfway down a side street. He didn't mention it because he knew she wouldn't have any idea what he meant. She might have thought she was supposed to feel sorry, and in her next letter, she would say that Tyler had no idea how bad she and her husband felt about the way things were and so on.

It was a good window, but he didn't really like it. There were a lot of people to see, but they all seemed very strange. He couldn't get used to them. Maybe it was because of Mrs. Bell. She was turning him against watching them.

But he felt the same way when he first moved into the other room, and the room before that. It always took him a long time to get used to a new room and its window. And then one day, he hoped, he would be looking out the window and it would occur to him that this window and this room were all right after all. He hoped it would happen soon. But it wouldn't. Maybe it would never happen because of Mrs. Bell and the dog.

He watched a car drive down the street and slowly turn the corner.

He stood in the chair looking out the window for a long time, not thinking, trying not to think, and now and then he spoke out loud, answering voices from memory. There were the time-softened faces of people he knew when he was in the handicapped school here in Chicago. He had had lots of fun in the handicapped school the four months he was there and he had known a lot of people there who would be his friend as long as he lived. He would never forget them. Sometimes he thought he would write a letter to Mrs. Gabree or Mrs. Malone or Mr. Holt who worked there. When he first left the handicapped school, he thought about them all the time. And Mrs. Gabree came to see him a couple of weeks after he left the school. She told him she didn't like what she saw, because Tyler wasn't doing anything, and at the handicapped school he had learned some things to do so he could make his own way. But she was impressed that he kept his room neat and straight, and she saw that he still had all the small furniture that had been made for him by others at the handicapped school. He would have written Mrs. Gabree a long time ago, except he was afraid that after she got his address she would come and see him again, and he would be embarrassed for her to come and see him now. And anyway, she probably didn't even work there at the handicapped school anymore. That was ten years ago.

He heard a noise downstairs and thought at first it was just Mrs. Bell coming in the back door. But then he heard different noises. He got down from the chair and put his shoes on. His first thought was that someone had followed him back here and they were going to come up and get him, for sometimes when he went out people followed him.

He listened. It sounded like there were a lot of people down in the kitchen. There was an awful lot of noise, a lot of feet, a lot of people hurrying around. He slowly went over to the door and put his ear to it. He held his arms in tight at his sides.

From downstairs he heard Mrs. Bell yelling.

Maybe a burglar had got in. Maybe a burglar had followed her. But wouldn't the dog stop a burglar? And Mrs. Bell was still yelling in the same mean way she did when she was fighting with the dog. Tyler wondered who she had brought home with her that she would be talking to that way, and still there was a lot of noise of feet down in the kitchen. Tyler turned the knob on his door and opened it slightly.

The noise down in the kitchen abruptly stopped. Which meant Mrs. Bell and whoever was with her had passed down the hall to the sitting room. Now he could hear them better. He pushed the door open wide enough for him to stick his head out and see the top of the stairs. Then he couldn't move.

The dog topped the stairs, its bright black eyes fixed on him as if it had been staring at the crack in the door even before Tyler opened it wider, and Tyler stood there as the dog came down the hall as if it were gliding, its feet not touching the floor, and Tyler couldn't look away and with both hands he tried to find the doorknob, still unable to look away from the dog as it now passed the bathroom door, not running but trotting lightly on its stiff long legs, its lips curled back from its teeth, its tongue lolling out

45

the corner of its mouth, hideous laughter on its sharp face, and he saw the chain dragging between its legs.

Still he couldn't move, couldn't even close his eyes, and then his hand found the doorknob and he drew his head back and the door swung shut with great slowness just as the dog reached it.

When the door was shut, he heard the growling and realized the dog had been growling as it came down the length of the hall. It scratched at the door, and its growling changed tone and went back and forth between a tight-throated, furious whining and an intense low snarl, a sound very much like the voice of a man.

Tyler backed away from the door and watched the knob. He was afraid the dog would — with horrible luck — strike the knob with a paw and turn it just enough to open the door.

He went to the side of the bed and started to climb up on it. He stopped. For what seemed like a long time he stared down at short, stubby arms, at his fat small hand gripping the bedspread.

Now the dog was scratching at the door. Tyler could see it, through the door, reared up on its hind legs.

He dropped down to his hands and knees and crawled under the bed, clear to the wall, and he backed up, looking out. He coughed from the dust he had stirred under the bed, and he put both hands over his mouth to stifle the coughing.

He lay on his side, looking at the floor of the room beyond the bed, and the scratching went on and on. Then he heard Mrs. Bell out in the hall yelling at the dog. The dog gave a sharp yelp, and Tyler heard the clinking of the chain. Then the door opened.

He closed his eyes and put his hands over his face.

But he had to look. He spread his fingers and looked. He saw the dog's legs and sharp feet flashing black as it came into the room, and then the black high-topped shoes of Mrs. Bell as she came in. The dog ran from the door to the far end of the room. Then its face suddenly appeared as it looked under the bed. Its eyes and its face had knowing in them. The dog growled, both black eyes staring up. It lowered itself awkwardly and started under the bed.

All the while Mrs. Bell was yelling at the dog, "See, nobody's in here, get back, get back there, what are you doing?" and its head was under the bed, and Tyler lay very calmly. He moved his hips forward slightly and kicked the dog in the side of the head as hard as he could. But it wasn't hard enough. The dog just blinked its eyes, stopped growling for a moment as it snapped its mouth closed, as if to swallow, and then its mouth opened again, wrinkling its black face and squinting its eyes tight, and Tyler drew both feet up under him to stomp at the dog's face, and when he did — this time kicking with both feet as hard as he could — he closed his eyes, and it was like jumping into a deep hole.

And then he was screaming and grabbing with both hands for the bedsprings, for the dog had one of his feet in its mouth and was shaking its head from side to side and snapping its mouth open and closed, trying to hurt, its eyes squinted nearly shut and looking up at Tyler's face now, right in the eye, and he tried to kick the dog's head with his other foot, aiming for the eye, and for a moment he heard his own cramped voice yelling, "Stop it. Stop it," and far in the distance he heard Mrs. Bell yelling.

The dog's head jerked down into the floor and the outer edge of the bed lifted slightly as the dog's back was banged up against it, and Tyler's shoe came off in the dog's mouth as Mrs. Bell dragged the dog from under the bed by the chain.

Tyler watched as Mrs. Bell kicked the dog, knocking it off its feet. It barked and then whined and snapped at her, and the shoe fell to the floor. Mrs. Bell kicked the shoe back under the bed, and Tyler stared at it as it lay on its side in front of him. It was wet. He held his nose to keep from sneezing and the dust was in his throat and lungs and he was going to cough, and he turned onto his stomach and pushed his face hard into his hand until he felt he was going to burst.

When he could breathe again, he turned his face to the side and saw Mrs. Bell's feet going to the door, and the stiff, resisting feet and legs of the dog as she dragged it out of the room.

Finally they were out of the door, then outside, and the door slammed.

He lay still, listening to her mumbling down the hall. He heard a door shut, then the heavy sound of her walking in the hall again, and his door suddenly opened.

"Yoo hoo," she yelled. "You can come out now. It's okay." She waited a moment, then he saw the door swing shut.

47

He reached over and got his shoe. He lay listening to the noises of the house. He heard her go into her room down the hall. He heard her talking to the dog. Then there was a long silence that was cut by the pure cold sound of the dog whining.

She came out of the room again, and he heard and felt the diminishing shake of the floor as she went down the hall to the stairs and then downstairs.

He stayed under the bed until night. He heard Mrs. Bell come back upstairs and go into her room for the night. She had another fight with the dog. He heard her talking to it; then she yelled at it. The dog growled and barked, and Tyler could even hear the powerful click as it snapped at her. Then there was the clinking of the chain and again the dog's piercing whine.

Tyler slowly came out from under the bed and climbed up into it, still in his clothes. He lay over against the wall, perfectly motionless. He pulled the covers over him, over his head. Now and then he pulled them down and looked out to see, in the light from the window, that the door of his room was still shut.

He got in the bed and took off his tie and shirt, but he didn't take his trousers off because he had to go to the bathroom and he didn't believe he could stand the moving around to get his pants off.

He lay awake, trying not to think, but the need to relieve himself became so great he had to get out of bed.

He stood in the center of the dark, large room for a while. He could risk going down the hall to the bathroom. But it was on the other side of Mrs. Bell's room, and he knew the dog would hear him. Mrs. Bell probably had her bedroom door shut. But he couldn't be sure of it.

His need to urinate was so great he had to hold himself, and for a moment he thought he would urinate in spite of himself, standing right there in the center of the room.

He thought of using the wastebasket. But that wouldn't work. And the window was too high, it would be dangerous, and someone going by, even if it was late, might look up and see him. Anyway, he probably couldn't open the big window.

He walked around in the dark room. For a while that helped, moving around. But then he had to stop and just stand there.

Then he thought of using the shirt he had just taken off. He reached over onto the bed and found the shirt.

He hesitated. But there was nothing else to do. He held the shirt wadded and urinated into it. He gritted his teeth.

When he finished, he stood holding the shirt, his hand wet. He went over and hung the shirt on the back of the rocking chair.

He bent down and wiped both hands on the rug and, not letting himself think, he got back into the big bed.

Maybe tomorrow Mrs. Bell would go out again and take the dog with her. Or she would have the two sisters next door come over to her house, and with the two sisters here she wouldn't be afraid of burglars and maybe she would put the dog back outside.

The day after tomorrow she would go out, and when she did, she would take the dog back outside. He hoped she would. If she didn't put it back outside, he didn't know what he would do. If she took it, he would leave the house and never come back. He would have to leave the rocking chair behind, but that didn't matter. It didn't look right anyway without the other furniture that went with it.

He would leave with his one suitcase and he would go somewhere else.

Tomorrow, while he was waiting to see if Mrs. Bell was going to leave with the dog, he would write his sister a letter and tell her what happened. It would be a long letter. He would tell her everything. But not about the shirt. He would never tell anybody about that.

He would have his suitcase already packed and when Mrs. Bell left, he would leave too. He would go to the post office first, just to take a look to see for sure he didn't have some mail, and from the post office maybe he would catch a city bus, though he didn't like to ride buses because of all the people.

He turned onto his side and stared at the window. What if Mrs. Bell went out tomorrow and left the dog inside the house?

He closed his eyes but continued staring straight ahead into darkness. After a while, as sleep eased the strain from his body, he watched himself rise and move almost silently through the hallway and down the back steps, the only sound that might give him away the clanking of the chain on his ankles, the loose end still dragging across his dream.

49

A LAMENT TO WOLVES

AGAIN ELLA'S HANDS TREMBLED. She looked away from Loren and the others, and put down her cup and saucer. She stood up, and they continued talking as she left the room.

In the kitchen she stood at the sink and looked out the window. Her hands were still. She saw his face, then, reflected gray in the window, and her hands trembled — the fingers tingling, cold, and a feeling like cold silk grazing the insides of her arms made her press them to her sides. Her mother hobbled into the kitchen. "Well, Ella, I don't guess you and Edmond would consider staying over tonight."

"No," she said. "Edmond gets up even earlier on Mondays than on the rest of the week. He's got a truckload of lumber that's supposed to come up from Tennessee, and he's having trouble with the hired hands. He just can't get them to work regular. And things pile up on weekends, so Mondays are bad."

Her mother went to the icebox as Ella spoke. Perhaps she listened to what Ella said. She got a pitcher of buttermilk. "Mondays. Mondays always have been bad days for me. It was a Monday your daddy got killed, and it was a Monday I had my stroke, and ..." She poured the buttermilk and held up the glass level with her old gray eyes. She stared at it as if she feared something was wrong with it.

She drank the whole glass of buttermilk without taking it from her thin-lipped mouth. With the tip of her tongue she licked at the thick white mustache it left on her lip. Staring out the window, she said, "But it was Monday a week tomorrow that I got the telegram from Loren saying he was still alive and he was coming home at last."

For a moment Ella thought her mother was praying, for her breath wheezed, and Ella could nearly hear the hissed whisper of the intense prayers her mother constantly uttered — though Ella had decided long ago, when she was a child, that they weren't truly prayers, that they weren't addressed to God, that they were just old-woman whisperings. She wasn't talking to herself; she didn't even know herself what she was saying. She was just mumbling.

In the other room, Loren, his wife Ringo, and Edmond laughed loudly. They were laughing, Ella knew, at something Loren said. Ella's mother wiped off the buttermilk with the back of her hand and shook her head from side to side. "Thank God the boy's turned out good. He's a good man, like his daddy was." Ella stared out the window.

"It's a miracle," her mother went on. "If you ask me, it's a miracle of God," and she was silent until the nervous movement of her lips resumed, the restless whispering.

"Well, let's go join the party," her mother said and she gave Ella a long look. And for a moment Ella was afraid of the knowing in her mother's look, afraid of what her mother knew. When her mother spoke again, her tone was so low it was almost inaudible — as if it were coming from that remote level of the old woman's mumbling — so low Ella even thought it perhaps wasn't her mother's voice at all. "You're glad your brother has come home, aren't you, Ella?"

"Yes." She knew it was a terrible thing to admit.

"Yes. Good. We should be thankful."

He left the same day their father was killed in the orchard, and Ella had stood in the barn loft and looked out and she had seen her father running toward the farm and people were chasing him. No. No one had been chasing him. What she had seen and what she had dreamed were tangled like the dead limbs of the trees in the orchard, and when she thought of what happened her hands and arms ached, and Loren had hurt her, he had held her underwater in the creek, straddled her, gripping her arms, and he held her under the water. He had kissed her and hurt her and held her under the water and then he went away and she was in the barn.

She followed her mother into the other room. Ella looked at Edmond. He sat listening to another of Loren's stories, and as Ella watched her husband, she saw his lips move slightly. Then his smile — the soft, boyish, gentle smile — as he laughed at Loren's story. She was afraid for Edmond, afraid for him to be here in the same room with Loren.

She sat down and tried not to listen.

"If you're a civilian employee you got it made. They can't get close to you because there ain't that many of you so you don't have to stay all in one place like the soldiers do, so we spread out, just wherever we want to be so it's good for us. And we can do all those other goodies that the military types can't, like Trick Three." His sharp eyes glistened. "We put up somethin and when we get done with it we wait around and if they're gonna move in ... we see if they're gonna move in or just squat out there and look, cause you can tell if they're out there, every time. I can smell em. I can smell them a thousand yards off.

"So we move off and wait and when they move in to take over the stuff we put in there, we zap it. Dynamite." He shook his huge, handsome head, his lips curled into a ferocious smile. "That's Trick Three. They set in the grass and let us build it and they go in and then we blow it up. We got lots of tricks like that. We call it tricks because they don't know what we're doin. Trick One is real nasty. We draw em in close when we're putting something up like pontoons and they're goin to jump us. See, they think we don't know they're there, so they come in real close, right up to the water so we can't get away. They see we don't have no dogs, so they don't think we can know they're there, because the dogs can smell them, the Army has dogs with them, but we don't. Because I can smell them. I can smell them more good than the dogs can."

He started chuckling, deep in his throat, and he looked at Ringo and the two of them laughed as if this part of the story had special meaning for them, and they laughed louder and louder, and Edmond (Like a boy, Ella thought, listening to a story about men and women and death, and laughing even though he doesn't understand) laughed and slapped his knee.

"So they crowd up, see, and we're just standing around workin. They think. But in the shed we got a big auger and we drill in the bank down twenty feet and we got air tanks we dump in, and then we radio in air strikes and then we go in the shed and we go down in the hole with the air tanks." He swallowed. "Just about time they think they'll jump us, splop! they get the old napalm mufuck. That's Trick One. We done that a couple times."

Ringo — huge, hugely voluptuous, big-breasted, long-legged, blond, her face strangely large, bloated, as if it had never stopped growing — Ringo was nearly as large as Loren himself. Together in the room they seemed unnaturally immense, and if they wanted to, they could stand up and destroy everything — the furniture, the ceiling, the entire house — destroy it all by simply standing and lifting their arms.

Ringo told about the girl who did her hair at the beauty shop in Bon Dok. The girl sometimes came to work with bandages on her arms and feet. Ella pictured the tiny Oriental climbing up on chairs and tables to reach Ringo's hair, stretching yellow reedlike arms to reach across Ringo's breasts, each the size of a human head ... One day the little girl wasn't at the beauty shop when Ringo came to have her hair done, and the old Frenchwoman who owned the shop told Ringo the girl had been captured in a raid north of the city. The little girl had been a terrorist. (Loren's laughter started, an ominous chuckling deep in his chest.) "They knew all along she was doing it," Ringo said. "I was the only one who didn't know it. And every other day that sweet little twat did my hair and we would have nice little chats in French, and she would give me a massage, and all the time she probably had a ball of plastic explosive sewed in her panties."

Ringo looked at Loren and they laughed violently, and Edmond laughed, shaking his head from side to side.

Ella glanced at Loren as he laughed, his head tilted back and his mouth open wide, showing his large, white teeth. She looked down at the floor.

Then she felt him staring at her. She turned to her mother. But the old woman sat smiling, her lips moving, whispering, not paying any attention, and it occurred to Ella that that was only natural: why should the old woman need to know what they were talking about? She sat smiling, her head turned to the side, looking out the front window at the orchard.

And still Ella felt Loren staring at her, and finally she looked at him. His eyes were steady. They were like black stones. She slowly put her hands in her lap and clasped them tightly together as the trembling began.

"Those women over there are somethin else," Loren said. He was speaking to her. He grinned slowly, his mouth exceedingly wide. "Oriental ginch," he said low. "They may be little, but that don't stop them. That makes it good. That makes it just right."

"Loren is a lover," Ringo said. Ella looked at her. Ringo stared blankly at Loren. There was great stillness in the way Ringo looked at him.

They were all silent, as if waiting. "Sis," Loren said. The word hung in the air like an odor. She turned slowly and looked at him. "Sis, it's funny the way fate is," he said. "You stayed here all your life, and me, I got scooted all around. Argentina. Panama. Africa. Cambodia. You name it, I done it. And the funny part is, if I ran into you in a bar in one of those little towns I'd just gone up to you and patted you on the ass and started up the old Lobas line."

"You wouldn't have found your sister in a bar," Ringo said softly, not to him, maybe to Ella. He ignored her. "... and you'd gone juicy like that." He snapped his large fingers, making a loud smack, as if he had struck her, and maybe it was a signal, for he got up, staring intently at her, his eyes not blinking, and he came slowly across the room. Extending his hand and crouching slightly as he approached, walking on his toes, he said, "And while the mariachis rattle their red little hearts ..." He took her hand and she slowly stood, her face stiff. She stared at the collar of his shirt. She could smell the musk, apple smell of his breath. When she was standing, he drew her against him, put his arm around her waist and held her tight against him, as if he would press her completely into him. He bent down and put his face to hers until their noses touched, her eyes nearly closed but still seeing the black liquid of his eyes, "... we would dance," he whispered, barely moving his thick lips, and he moved her, turned, and they danced. "And we would talk and get friendly." He moved his head from side to side, rubbing his nose against hers.

"... some music on the radio," Ella heard her mother say from a great distance. She and Loren stood there together, his arm around her waist, heavy, and his unblinking eyes didn't look away from her.

There was music and they started moving again. "Slowly," he whispered. "Slow. Make it last. Make it last," and she breathed hard. He was holding her too tightly, the room was hot, she was weak, she would die, and as she took a deep breath, the air was hot, it was his breath, and she knew he was breathing into her, their lips nearly touching. He turned his head to the side. "Edmond. Dance with Ringo. She's a great dancer. Great. Just don't let her get in your pants is all. Eh, Ringo? Eh?"

She didn't answer, but stood up and went over to Edmond. "Come on," she said.

Loren turned his face back to Ella and put his cheek to hers, his lips touching her ear, and he whispered, "You're nice, Ella. Real nice. I mean it.

Ella. I never did think about you all this time. You know? Ella. Huh. Like Cinderella. I guess everybody says that to you, uh? Like a guy I know his name was John Kennedy and everybody wants to shake his hand. But you're nice, Ella. Real nice, and you know what I mean nice? Huh?" She couldn't speak. "I mean you're nice like it'd be a treat to kiss you. You know, slow, easy, just soft and easy . . ." And moving his lips along her cheek to her mouth, he slowly put his lips to hers, lightly, and he moved his lips back and forth until her lips hurt, were open, and he touched her lips with his tongue. Slowly back and forth it traced her lower lip, her upper lip, and her lips came together on his tongue and his tongue slid into her mouth.

And immediately out again before she could make herself think, and he turned his head to the side, then turned away from her, his arm brushing her hips as it moved down from her waist, and he talked to Ringo and Edmond, and Ella blinked and held her breath. Among the old dark furniture, the darkening windows, the walls closing in, she saw her mother sitting beside the radio, smiling, her eyes closed.

Ringo and Edmond stopped dancing and listened as Loren talked to them. Ella didn't hear what he said. Then Edmond was in front of her, talking, his round face intent, and she heard him saying, "... then just go ahead and stay if you'd like to. There's no reason I can see for you to come back today when you can just as easy wait till tomorrow. Since it's been so long since you've seen your brother."

Ella blinked at him. Loren took her arm and guided her away from Edmond toward Ringo, and Ringo, her face cold, her eyes large and blank, reached out to her. Ella obediently lifted her hand and let Ringo lead her to the bedroom where Loren and Ringo had slept last night.

Ringo closed the door and sat down on the bed. She took off her high heels and her hose. She stood up and went out of the room.

Ella stood before the old, time-bent mirror on the dressing table. She saw Loren in her face: the nose, mouth, and eyes — especially the eyes. All her life this face had been hers and not hers; she had known her face and not known it at all. And now she was knowing. It was coming up slowly, dark and wet, a reflection from a mirror placed far beneath the surface of water. She and Loren were the same flesh. She had believed this was gone, but it wasn't gone. Neither was gone the day when she stood in the door of the barn loft and looked out at the orchard and saw her father come running toward the house, his head and face and his shirt and overalls glistening red. From that day on Loren and most of her life were gone — though she saw, in the crooked mirror, that when he left she had gone with him and now she was back again, and she was now at last seeing herself.

It happened again, with her looking in the mirror: in the morning of that day Loren dragged her to the barn and that afternoon of the same day she got to her feet and looked out the door of the loft and just then she heard the shouting far away in the orchard. She thought the cows had jumped the fence and were into the orchard again and that Loren and her father were driving them out, and she forgot herself and looked out and in the distance ... or was it near? She couldn't know what she had seen and what she had deduced, maybe even invented by later thinking about it again and again, through long nights that were so silent now that both men, with their snoring that shook the small house, were gone.

She heard the car start — her and Edmond's car — and she went to the bedroom window and pulled the shade aside. Edmond was in the car, Loren was standing beside it. Stiffly, Edmond raised his hand and waved to her. It seemed he had been waiting for her to look out at him, as if Loren, who in his way knew all things, had told him that Ella would be looking out in a few moments and that he should wave good-bye to her when she did.

She watched as Edmond drove out of the barn lot, and she watched as the car slowly moved onto the gravel road and drove away. Loren walked toward the house.

She took down her dress and stepped out of it.

Ringo came back into the room. She had taken off her makeup. Her face was exceedingly pale, and she held her head down. "Put this on." She handed Ella a silk dress — green, orange, and red.

Ella's hands burned when she touched it.

"It'll fit you. Loren got it for me. He likes it. It hooks at the side. Like a sarong. It fits all sizes."

Ringo turned away and took off her dress. Her body was immense and white. She put on a full-length tight black dress with long sleeves. She stood at the mirror and took off the large, elaborate blond wig. Beneath it her hair was black and slick. She put the wig in a box and shoved it under the bed. From under the bed she took another, smaller box. It contained a black turban, which she put on her head.

When she was finished, she turned from the mirror. "Get dressed." She crossed the room to Ella and took the silk dress from her hand.

She stepped behind Ella and unsnapped her brassiere. Ella tried to hold it up to her breasts, but Ringo jerked the straps off her shoulders and pulled it away. She stepped in front of her, and though Ella held her head down, she could tell Ringo was looking at her breasts, first one, then the other. Then she looked down at Ella's slip. "Take that off. Everything. With this dress you wear nothing," and she watched while Ella obeyed.

Naked, still standing with her head down, Ella stared at the floor, then at her breasts, waiting for Ringo to speak. But she said nothing and Ella looked at Ringo's feet, at the sharp-toed black shoes beneath the long black dress, and slowly she raised her head, looking up the length of Ringo, and when she was to Ringo's face she forgot herself, her nakedness.

Ringo's face was stone gray, and it was as gaunt and drawn as the face of the old woman in the other room who sat by the radio with her eyes closed, dreaming of her son, while her son sat, panting, across the room from her.

The three of them went to town to Zeppels, then to Troy's Bar, and then they drove ten miles to the next town, stopped at roadhouses along the way, and then they went to all the bars in the next town.

Ringo drove the car and Ella and Loren rode in the back. She stared out the window at the night. He pulled her toward him and she lay against him. He unhooked the dress and opened it and laid his hand on her breast over her heart. Her breast raised and lowered her breast under his hand. The night slid by the window.

At another town, at another bar, they danced and when they didn't dance they sat side by side in a booth and he talked to her. He talked to her constantly, and his hand was on her under the table. Across the table Ringo sat.

They left and went out to the car and when she got into the back seat she reached out to him and again he unhooked her dress and she writhed and scooted in the seat until she was out of the dress. Ringo drove the car down a perfectly straight road, on and on, and they met no cars, they passed no towns, farmhouses; there was complete darkness beyond the pavement grayed by the headlights of their car, and the car was then descending through the night. It was going straight down.

Then she believed she saw flickers of light in the black. She blinked her eyes, waited.

She saw it again, as if something was running alongside the car — perhaps a great gray dog, or a gray horse, or a man dissolving.

She sat up, her face to the window, and the flickering was more distinct.

They were driving down the orchard road. It was the back road that came up from the river and passed through the orchard.

They were going incredibly fast. But the orchard road was bumpy, an old road unused except, years ago, during the harvest of the apples. But the car moved smoothly.

She looked up and saw the gray trees, row on row, blurring by the window, and she fell back slowly as she realized the car wasn't on the orchard road, but that they were in the orchard itself, they were sliding down the long, long row straight toward the barn, and she rose and looked over the black shoulder of Ringo. Ahead, in the distance, somehow visible, but dimly, beyond the cold swath of light from the headlights, framed in the point of the narrowing V of gray trees, she saw the house and the barn, and in the barn, though it was still a great distance away, she saw the loft door was open and she closed her eyes just as she began to see the small white outline of a girl crouching in the loft door, looking out.

The car stopped. She lay with her eyes closed. She listened and heard nothing. Then Ringo spoke low, in a strange language, not a language but a whine, rising and falling. Then she got out of the car and quietly shut the door.

Ella turned and tried to see Loren's face.

"Let's go," he said and lifted her until she was standing outside the car, and she saw their mother's house hovering in the darkness.

She followed him into the house. He left the room dark and turning to her, pushed the dress off her shoulders. She stood with her arms to her sides, waiting.

"Father was buried on the hill back of the orchard," she heard herself saying. She closed her eyes. "Do you remember the orchard the way it used to be? One time you and I were in a tree, all the trees running out from it in long lines. We were in the top and everything was silent and nothing was moving. It was like nothing had ever happened and nothing was ever going to happen. Everything was gone, and we were even different people. We weren't even people. When father was killed, you left and never came back."

He pulled her down to the floor.

"I wrote you letters and gave them to Mother and I guess she read them first before she put them away, or threw them away, I don't know, but then I guess she stopped reading them. Maybe I ought to ask her if she kept them. It would be interesting to … But they would be sad. Maybe even you would think they were sad if you read them. They were like love letters. And I knew they were love letters. That ought to please you. But maybe I wrote them as much to Father as to you, even if I put your name on them and it was you I was talking to." He began kissing her neck, her breasts.

"I couldn't sleep for a long time. Mother couldn't either. We got up again and again, every night. Mother would tell me I should go to sleep and I said I would and then we'd go back and lay awake in bed. Always I could hear the wind blowing in the orchard. Sometimes I still have a nightmare, and I see a man running down in the orchard. I call Mother to the back door and when she gets there the man turns off the row he was running down and he runs through the trees and we look down the rows and he is running toward the house, he is coming toward us … and I know … at the back of my mind I know it's … the man who killed Father, but I don't say it to Mother. But the minute I see him running toward the house I know it's the man who killed him... Loren, where were you? Why didn't you help Father? Where were you?"

He answered by slowly spreading her legs.

"Do you think of death as you travel in the same skin with it, even in sleep, an animal with lives like unending memories? Or does being death take it back to meaning nothing?" He lowered his head. He pierced her with his tongue. She stopped.

She opened her eyes to the dark room. The ceiling was streaked with gray lines. Without words, with nothing, she felt what he was doing and she heard herself moaning and she stopped herself. She lay there, listening to the sounds he was making. Finally he stopped.

Apart from her, somewhere in the darkness, he seemed to hide.

Then she saw him in the gray light emerging naked from the darkness as if he were stepping out of a black door, and he came slowly toward her, his hands at his sides, and he was swollen enormous, a fist on a forearm.

Ella was at the stove pouring another cup of coffee when Ringo came out of the bedroom. She said good morning to Ella's mother, glanced at Ella, and sat down at the table.

Ella's mother went on talking about when she and Ella's father came to this part of the country. They had two different families of children before Ella and Loren were born, and those two bunches of children had gone away, she didn't know where all they had gone, and most of them were old by now, had grandchildren of their own. The old woman laughed and said it seemed that those other children of hers were older than she was, much older.

Ella left the stove and sat at the table across from Ringo. Ringo looked at her and said, "Did you have fun last night?" Her face was again large, bright and smooth, but puffed by the layers of make-up.

Ella looked away. Her mother was now talking about all the children who had died. There had been at least two, three bunches of children who had died over the years.

"He'll stay in bed all day," Ringo said, her voice below the steady drone of the old woman's voice. "He's not sleeping. But he'll stay in there. But don't try to go in to him. He wouldn't like that. And later on, maybe this afternoon, he'll call me and I'll go in to him. You see how it is?"

Ella stared at her. The gray irises of Ringo's eyes had tiny cracks of black. They were like cinders. She had seen everything. She had traveled with Loren and she had seen everything he did. She loved it, and she would stay with him until, eventually, he killed her.

"Are you bleeding?" she whispered. Ella didn't answer. She looked away, then said, "Yes."

Ringo nodded, pleased, and lit a cigarette. She leaned back, folding her arms under her breasts. The long cigarette drooped in a corner of her mouth, and the eye above it squinted against the slow line of smoke loving across her face. "He killed a girl once," she said.

Ella's mother went on, chantlike.

"A Korean girl. He paid twenty dollars for her. We were in Pusan doing salvage. He paid her family twenty dollars for her and took her into tire warehouse and killed her." She smiled slowly. "I guess you know how. You know." Her tone changed. She spoke without the flat hardness of before. Now it was too far the opposite, chatty, and as she talked, the cigarette in her mouth wobbled, bobbed up and down, and spilled ashes. "You know, it's really amazing. I've never seen another one like it. Anywhere. Have you?" Ella didn't answer. "The first time I saw it ... I remember. I didn't think it was real. It's amazing." She paused, staring at Ella. "And you're his sister." She laughed.

Then her tone changed again. Her eyes dimmed. The cigarette had burned down almost to her lips. "That don't matter to him. He likes it all." She took the cigarette from her lips and looked at it, then ground it out in the saucer of Ella's cup. "Why did he kill his old man?" she said.

The room roared with coldness. The silence was like glass around the three of them, and Ella knew her mother had been listening and knew — had been listening all along and knew everything — and the glass of silence was broken when Ella and her mother spoke at the same time, the old woman chanting loudly, or moaning in her old-woman, animal way, and Ella heard herself saying, "He didn't kill Father. That isn't what happened. It's wrong."

But Ringo wasn't listening. She had lit another cigarette and now sat with her eyes squinted closed, and Ella knew she was gone back to all those places where terrible things happened and she was trying to undo, in the way of a woman (in that part of her that was still a woman), all those things, trying to make them better by recreating them from their memories — just as he recreated them, not merely in reverie but in his violent action, each time again making the same error, each time at the fatal moment plunging over into that loose dark air where everything happens. Ella was talking, saying what for years she had dreamed, saying she looked out the loft door and saw her father and he was bleeding, he was torn, he had been chopped, and the man chasing him with a hatchet in each hand was not Loren, that the man had been too far away for her to see, and there hadn't been a man there at all, her father had fallen under the harrow. Her mother was looking at her through the room buzzing with words like flies. Her mother's eyes were sharp, clear.

The afternoon was as bright, as yellow, as fire, as if she and her mother had just now come back into the kitchen from the field, sweating, and his blood soaked through their dresses, her mother's face wet with sweat but calm.

They were silent, the old woman choked on her prayers, Ringo gone, in Panama, Brazil, Korea, Vietnam. Ella sat there, still feeling him, and for a long time the only sound was the wind, far away, in the orchard.

Then the old woman was looking out at the orchard again, and she started talking, on and on, about the families she had given birth to, and from the other room they heard him.

He called low, not uttering the name but growling. Ringo got up and walked slowly to the bedroom door, waited, then entered.

Ella listened, and then the noise began. The old woman, oblivious in time, talked, and though she talked, perhaps she heard the sounds from the bedroom. Perhaps she felt the rattling vibrations that shook the house, and perhaps she heard beneath her droning their strong, urgent voices like the snarling voices of wolves.

When the house stopped shaking there was a long silence.

The old woman slept in her chair by the window, her head hanging.

And later, after the long day, Ella heard the car coming down the road. She calmly went out of the house.

Edmond waved to her and got out of the car, a breath of vapor wisping from the overheated engine block. When he slammed the door, the car shook and sunlight moved in the long teeth of the grille, making the chromium gleam. Edmond was talking excitedly about what had happened — Walter's truck had broken down at Richmond, and Edmond and Lloyd had to go down and unload it and get another truck, and Carl Johnson had called in the afternoon and said he would lease Edmond the lot next to the store but Edmond would have to do the building himself, and Edmond was going to have Ella talk to the Smith girls again about their father and his loan . . .

At first what he said came from far off. But Ella began slowly recognizing the names and then suddenly she knew what he was saying. She answered him, hardly hearing herself. With her first words, she saw Edmond leaning in to her, listening intently now that this part of him was back. Behind them, the grille was grinning at everything she said, its wide mouth open, steam still licking from under the hood.

THE ANGEL BUSINESS

ONE DARK AFTERNOON a taxi came down the road. I rose from my desk and went to the window. The car stopped and the driver, an old man, walked around and opened the back door.

A large man got out. When he had straightened to his full height, I recognized my old school chum, Russell. I could hardly believe my eyes.

We stood before the fire and toasted the past. Russell's hair was gray, but he was still robust. He talked loudly and often interrupted himself with braying laughter which rattled through the empty house. I told him I had given up. He seemed not to hear. He talked on, and his face relaxed — his forehead unwrinkled, and his cold blue eyes were as clear and intense as when we were boys. "To great things!" he shouted and struck his glass against mine, nearly shattering them. We drank. Then — "To success!" We drank.

"I say, Russell," I put in quickly, "what have you been doing all these years?"

He clenched his teeth. His face bloated. "A total waste. But I hunt ..."

"And that's why you've come out here?"

Then he whispered, "There were business ventures."

"Tell me, " I said. "I'm quite interested."

He looked at me sharply. "You are? Why? You said you had given up. Anyway, you should know about failure."

"How did you know. Who told you?"

"It doesn t matter." He turned away. In a mirror across the room I saw his face dimly reflected. He was grinning hideously.

But when he turned to me, his expression was blank. "Let's forget the past," he said calmly. "I am married. Did you know?"

"Of course not. Congratulations."

"Actually it's the second time. My first wife died."

"Oh. I'm sorry."

"Don't be. She didn't die. I killed her. Shot her with my bow and arrow."

He exploded with laughter and slapped me on the shoulder. "To the future!" he shouted.

We drank. "Will I have the pleasure of meeting the new Mrs. Russell?"

"By and by." His face sagged, darkened. It seemed tremendously thick, as if layered with clay. His eyes shifted beneath his brows. "I'm on to something," he whispered.

"Good." When he didn't go on, I added: "I will help if I can, if that's what you want. If it's a matter of money."

"You don't understand," he said darkly.

"What is it?'

"Angels."

"Oh. Angels?"

I waited. The pause lengthened: we faced each other, disappearing into ourselves in the fading light. "My good friend," I said, "please stay. I am glad you have come. You will find peace here, as I have. The solitude. . ."

A servant entered the room. The man arrogantly looked at me and announced dinner was served.

Russell laughed and pounded me on the back. "He's part of my staff," he said. "The others are on their way." He pointed to the window — the taxi was coming up the driveway. Through the darkness I saw the car was filled with shadows that could easily have been people.

In the dining room the long table was set for two. From the kitchen entered more servants, carrying trays.

One of them announced Mrs. Russell had arrived.

"Good," Russell said. He sat down and motioned for me to take the other place. I obeyed, and then asked, "Won't Mrs. Russell join us for dinner?"

Russell shook his head. "Let us save that for later, shall we?"

The servants' procession continued until the table was piled high with food.

We sat before the fire in the study. Perhaps this was the time: "Russell," I said, "I want to talk to you about my work here, why I have given up, why I have lived out here all these years. Surely you have wondered."

He leaned forward. "Ahh," he said.

But he wasn't-looking at me. A figure in white emerged from the shad-

65

ows. She was tall and thin, with orange hair standing on end. Her skin was milky white. A violet vein pulsed at her temple, and the same faint violet traced her throat. She carried a little white ball. Looking at neither of us, she bit into it. A cookie! Slowly, meditatively, she ate it. She brushed the crumbs from her fingertips and pulled a ribbon at her throat. Her gown dropped. The room was silent except for the pop and hiss of the fire. She knelt and bent forward onto her elbows.

A snort echoed in the room. Russell had stood and was taking off his trousers.

The next morning Russell came downstairs and cheerfully insisted 1 join him for breakfast.

"No, Russell," I said firmly.

"Oh, 1 say. You're embarrassed about last night." He brayed.

I refused to look at him.

"Come on, old fellow," he said. "You must eat. Even you eat." He linked his arm in mine and pulled me to the dining room.

"Today is the day!" he roared down the table at me.

When we finished, Russell's servants brought in heavy trousers, hunting jackets, and Russell's bow and arrows. We donned the hunting clothes and went outside where the taxi waited. The old man tipped his hat and opened the car door. Then above us a loud firm voice commanded: "Russell!"

"Yes, love," Russell answered. A huge woman stood on the balcony. She wore a green velvet dress with gold piping and black ruffles. Her face was deeply wrinkled, and her steep forehead was topped by a helmet of gray hair.

"Wait for Dr. Horace," she said.

"Very well. And you, my dear? Will you join us?"

She turned and went into the house.

"Who was that?' I asked.

"My wife. Pardon me for not introducing you."

Out of the house came a little man wearing a black top hat, black cape, black suit, and black patent leather slippers. Under his arm he cradled a shotgun. "Good morning," he said curtly, looking at neither of us. He went straight to the taxi and got into the back seat.

"This is Dr. Horace — Eunice's husband," Russell said.

"I believe you met my wife last night," the doctor said, looking at me.

"Shall we be off?" Russell said. He and I got in beside the driver.

We followed the dirt road into the woods. The farther we drove, the more worried I became about the shotgun. At last I glanced over my shoulder ...

The little doctor was sprawled in the seat, knees wide apart. His head hung forward and his hat had fallen off, exposing a skull wisped with dull brown hair. His open cape and coat revealed his shirt, stained with blots of pale green, purple, and the same orange of Eunice's hair.

I leaned toward Russell. "Dr. Horace is having a nap."

Russell shook his head. "He swoons. It's the opium muffins. He and Eunice are devotees."

The road narrowed to a path, and the driver stopped the car. On the cold air floated the pellucid voices of birds.

Russell stalked through the woods. I followed, and behind me trailed Dr. Horace. As if charmed, animals came trotting straight to Russell, and he shot them with his bow. We dragged the dead beasts behind us.

Dr. Horace dropped farther back. The last time I looked over my shoulder, he was lying down in the leaves.

Late that afternoon when we returned, servants unloaded the game from the back seat of the taxi. They heaved out the stag, partridges, the boar, turkeys, hares, ducks, and the black bear onto the dusty ground. The pile stood higher than the taxi. I stuck my head into the car: the back seat was drenched with blood.

Russell and I went into the study and were having a drink when Mrs. Russell entered.

She stood a head taller than Russell and I — and that head was three hands wide, with a face chalk-white except for two red dots on her cheeks. Her eyes were nearly closed under thick eyelids as she spoke: "Professor Koch, his wife, and daughter have arrived."

Russell turned to me. A gloating smile came to his face and crept too far in both directions, revealing his jagged teeth. "My good man," he whispered, "I do hope you won't refuse us."

"Refuse you?"

"You have been awfully good so far."

"Feel quite free, Russell. But as for myself ..." I turned away.

"No more of that!" he shouted. "Remember, I'm bringing you to life." He laughed loudly, his mouth wide.

Eight of us sat down to dinner: the Russells, Dr. Horace and Eunice, myself, and the Koch family — the Professor, bald, obese, perspiring; his small wife, constantly whispering to herself; and their adolescent daughter, skinny as a stick, her blue paper eyes staring across the table at Dr. Horace. The conversation turned to angels.

"I would like to believe you, Russell," Professor Koch said. "But you can't blame me for being skeptical."

Russell laughed, squinting intensely. "Skeptical! Wait until you see."

"See," Koch said.

"Of course," Dr. Horace said. "We're quite prepared."

"Oh," Koch said to Dr. Horace. "You are Russell's colleague in this venture." Koch turned to me. "And you?"

I shook my head. "1 know nothing of it."

"He hasn't asked you to invest?"

Russell interrupted: "1 asked no one to invest." He glared at Mrs. Koch, busily whispering to herself — "Must you do that?"

She froze.

Russell went on: "I ask no one for money. Angels aren't impressed by money."

"Very well, Russell," Koch said, "let's get on with it."

As we were leaving the dining room, Koch's daughter caught my attention and with her lips silently enunciated Wait. The others went into the study. The girl sternly asked me, "Is it true about Mr. Russell?"

"Is what true? Frankly, I'm lost."

"Is it true he has powers?"

"Russell? Powers? Why, I ..." I hurried past the girl when I realized that if I looked only a little deeper into the strange dry blue of her eyes I would make a horrible discovery.

The others sat in a half-circle facing Russell. We joined them. "Angels," Russell said.

Koch spoke: "Bona fide angels, or local spirits? This is fairy country."

"Big white angels," Russell said.

"What proof have you?"

Mrs. Russell rose. "We have a plethora of proof," she said, barely opening her eyes. "Enlarged glands ..."

"Photographs," Russell corrected her.

"Enlarged photographs. Plaster casts of footprints. Large fingerprints which have no swirls or whorls" — she lifted her arm, her big hand spiraling upward.

"And of course we have the best proof of all," Russell said. "The angels themselves."

I spoke: "There are angels here?"

"Precisely!" Russell answered.

Servants wheeled in a table bearing a display: a plaster print of a large, five-toed foot with a horn-like projection at the heel — a talon, Russell called it; a dozen photographs. Dr. Horace's work: foggy shots of a figure in white. In one picture the angel was coming headfirst through the wall for what was certain to be a very awkward landing at the foot of the stairs. And there were fingerprints, made by fingers large as sausages.

Russell led us into the hall to the spot where the angel had flown through the wall. "Here," Russell said. "His handprint."

In the post at the foot of the stairs a smooth handprint was sunk two inches into the marble. "Apparently the fellow leaned on it," Koch mumbled.

"Notice the size," Russell said. "Sixteen inches from the base of the hand to the tip of the middle finger."

I stepped forward and put my hand into the impression. When I touched the stone I felt a strange warmth.

In the study again, Russell informed us that last evening he and Mrs. Russell, while strolling in the garden, had met an angel among the rose bushes. "Hello, there," the angel said, and had talked to them for several hours.

Russell went on, but at that point I slipped out the nearest French door. I crossed the terrace and went into the garden.

The sky was dusty with stars, and the cold scent of flowers filled the air. A mist lay in the garden and as I walked along the path it was as though 1 were wading in a pond. I lit a cigar and waited.

Nothing happened.

Naturally. Russell knew how to do a thing. I thumped away the cigar. But as I was leaving the garden, I felt someone close behind me.

I refused to turn. I went up onto the terrace. Then I felt as if I was being watched — not by the person in the garden, but by others. Perhaps Russell and the rest were watching from the black windows of the house.

I woke shouting and shaking my fist at Russell. I was in bed, and the light of day filled the room. I lay a while in the deep silence of my house.

Then outside the door there was a commotion — people running, shouting.

I dressed quickly and unlocked my door. A young servant came running down the hall at top speed. I grabbed his arm. "Let me go," he said, rolling his eyes.

"What's the trouble?" I yelled in his face.

"Emergency! Mr. Russell!"

Downstairs, servants rushed about. "What is happening?" I called.

"Are you ready for breakfast, sir?" A round-faced maid appeared before me.

"I don't want breakfast, my dear. I want to know what the trouble is."

"The Koch family, sir," the girl said. She was very pretty — round cheeks and clear eyes. "Something awful has happened."

After asking her name — Rose! — I hurried down the corridor to Koch's suite. It was full of smashed furniture and shattered plaster. A huge hole was torn in a corner. In the center of the room Professor Koch was tending to his wife, who was badly battered. Their daughter — naked from the waist up — sat on a pile of debris, while Dr. Horace dreamily globbed salve on a bruise in the center of her bony chest.

"What happened?" I asked.

"Big snakes," Dr. Horace said and winked.

Koch turned from his wife. "Giant boa constrictors tore into the house and attacked us," he said. "Thank goodness Russell came when he did. He saved our lives."

At that moment Russell entered from the next room. "Just look," he said, rolling up his shirt sleeves. Large snakebites tracked both arms. They resembled red hoof prints.

"But I killed one," Russell said. "I fought three at once and crushed the head of one. Like this" — he clasped his hands. "Its head burst," he shouted. "Blood squirted out. It was like a fire hose."

"After the attack," Koch said, "the other snakes dragged off the dead one."

"Astounding!" I exclaimed. "How many were there in all?"

"A baker's dozen," Koch's daughter answered, and pushed away Dr. Horace's hand.

Rose was waiting outside. "Come this way, sir," she whispered and took my hand. We tiptoed down the hall.

She sat me at the kitchen table and served breakfast. The servants one by one were sneaking out the back door, carrying their bags. "And what about you, my dear?" I asked Rose.

"I wouldn't leave you, sir." Her eyes were large and deep.

"And what will come of all this?" I asked.

"Mr. Russell won't back down," she said. "That is certain. He will go on and on. Until the worst."

When I left the kitchen I saw Professor Koch's back as he went out the front door. I followed.

At the foot of the steps Koch was waving at the taxi coming down the road. His wife and daughter leaned against each other. Mrs. Koch saw me and came over. "We must leave," she said with animation, her eyes flashing. "The Professor has had second thoughts about this angel business." We looked at the Professor. He stared across the road into the woods. Mrs. Koch stepped closer to me and whispered low, "If I were you, I would give it up. Mr. Russell is insane, but this time he is onto something."

"He is? What?" I asked.

"The Professor believes Mr. Russell has become an angel."

The cab turned up the driveway. The old driver stumbled out and loaded the bags into the trunk. The Kochs got in and drove off without waving, without even looking back.

At dinner Rose served the five of us. We were silent through the meal. Russell sat brooding at the head of the table.

At last Mrs. Russell spoke. "The Kochs left just when matters were becoming clear."

"The Kochs cannot be blamed," Russell said. "Plainly, those snakes were a put-up job. The sort of thing an angel just can't resist."

"The Kochs are cowards."

"My dear Mrs. Russell," Dr. Horace said, slumping so low in his chair he seemed about to slide under the table. "I'm a coward and I have remained. Let's give credit where credit is due, shall we?"

She ignored this and said to Russell, "Tonight we must try."

He seemed not to hear. Then without looking up, he said, "No. There's too much against it."

"But we've come this far."

"Maybe too far."

"If you refuse, I shall without you," she said.

"Very well. Tonight." He looked across the table at me. "Are you with us?"

"I suppose so," I said. "But what exactly is it we're going to do?"

They stared at me — even Rose, standing behind Russell's chair. "Why," Russell said slowly, "we shall ... seize it."

"Oh. Well then — yes. Count me in."

We were stationed at strategic locations through the house where the angel might appear. My location was on the balcony overlooking the front lawn and the road. I was equipped with a walkie-talkie, and armed with a bow and arrows, as was Russell. It was his theory that angels could be intimidated by these weapons — and these only.

The night was clear and cold under the moon. I faced the silent forest across the road.

It was well past midnight. Now and then a voice cheeped from my walkie-talkie. I leaned against the wall. Wind moved through the forest . . .

The walkie-talkie woke me — not with the piping voice of one of the others, but with an urgent spizz of static.

I spoke into the walkie-talkie. Nothing. I shook it, struck it, but received no reply.

I hurried off the balcony and inside. I ran down the dark corridor, my footsteps echoing.

I stopped, holding my breath and listening.

Black silence. Then laughter — far away.

I hurried from room to room, but didn't find Russell and the others.

I again listened. At first, nothing. Then again the distant laughter. But somewhat louder. Then the voices were gone. I waited in the darkness.

Again I heard them — in the next room!

I rushed down the hall to the dining room. But it was empty. I held my breath. Silence.

I returned to the study ...

And heard their voices, distinctly now, from the wall separating the study and the dining room.

I approached the wall which was covered with a ceiling-high bookcase. I stood near it. I heard them talking and laughing.

With my face nearly touching the books, I moved down the bookcase. I stopped. I could nearly make out the words the tiny voices spoke.

I took a book from the shelf. In its empty space I saw a room and they were sitting in a circle — Russell, Mrs. Russell, Dr. Horace and Eunice, and Rose!

I started to call to them.

But then Russell lifted both arms and stood. He crossed the circle and stood before Rose.

I wanted to turn away, but couldn't. Though Rose turned her head, she stood and stepped forward.

"Don't," I whispered. "Please don't." She began undressing.

Russell stripped ... and Professor Koch was correct! Naked, Russell looked like a huge white pigeon.

I replaced the book. I turned to the windows, silver and hard with moonlight.

"Bad luck last night," Russell said the next morning when he came into the dining room where I sat alone. "No angels hereabouts, after all." He reached down and took a strip of bacon from my plate.

Rose came in, carrying a tea pot. When she saw Russell, she looked down and mumbled.

"Speak up, girl," Russell said.

"Would you care for breakfast, sir?"

"No," he said. "Haven't time." Turning to me, he extended his hand. "I hope my stay has been as edifying for you as it has been pleasant for me."

"Indeed," I said and stood.

We walked down the hall to the door. "Mrs. Russell, Dr. Horace and Eunice left early this morning," he said.

"You've done everything," I said.

"Yes. Everything is taken care of," Russell said quite busily.

"But not quite," I said.

"What's that?"

We stood on the steps. The black taxi waited in the driveway.

"There's the matter of Rose," I said, and he glanced at me.

"Oh." He chuckled. "So you know. Well." His shoulders lifted in a huge shrug. "I hardly know what to say."

"Will you be taking her with you?"

He looked at me with puzzlement and something like disappointment — or offense. "No. Why should I?"

I nodded once and looked away.

"I say," he went on. "1 hope this won't come between you and me."

"Only somewhat."

"That's more like it. Time cures, they say." He stepped nearer, again we shook hands, and while he skipped down the steps I turned and reached into the umbrella stand inside the door.

At the cab he turned to wave. I shot. The arrow struck him in the chest. He fell into the back seat of the taxi, which lurched forward, slamming the door. The car drove down the road.

Of course I didn't shoot him — though I had entertained several variations of the scene before Russell came downstairs, said good-bye, got in the taxi, and rode off, waving out the rear window.

When the car disappeared down the road and the sound of its motor died, I went into the house. "Rose," I called. My voice echoed deep into the house.

I went into my study, lit a cigar, and stood at the window. The sky was low and the forest awaited the burials of winter.

I turned to my desk. Soon Rose's sister was by my side — her name was Lily. She lit a cigarette and let it dangle in the corner of her mouth. "I like that," she whispered, and put her hand on my shoulder.

HOUSE HUNTING NEAR THE FRONTIER

WE WALKED UP THE STEPS OF THE BIG HOUSE. From the porch we could see the city, tiny in the distance.

Father unlocked the front door with the key he had got from the real estate people, and we went in.

The room was vast and empty. There was nothing for us to look at but its largeness and the fireplace. Mother started talking. She immediately understood the house and how she felt about it. The next thing was to make Father feel the same way. While Mother talked to Father we walked through the other rooms on the first floor and came to a large staircase. We started up, and the stairs went on and on. We stopped to catch our breath, turning and looking back at the room far below. We reached the second floor and a wide hall with hundreds of doors. We started down the hall. We walked and walked but it seemed to me we were getting nowhere. Father apparently had the same feeling because he started complaining. But as usual he didn't complain about the right thing. (I never understood that in Father: it was as if he were hiding from himself.) This time he chose to complain about me.

Mother became interested in what he was saying. She agreed with him, though she admitted the particulars Father brought up hadn't occurred to her. But clearly Father had given considerable thought to the matter. Mother pitched in and the two of them complained heartily about me as we went down the endless hallway, with me in the middle. Then we came to another stairs, and fell silent.

The staircase was little wider than a person's hips, and each step was cut shallowly. Climbing these stairs would be like going up a ladder.

Father pointed at the stairs and looked at me. I started climbing. Looking down between my feet I saw Father was following, and Mother was somehow climbing after him.

We went up and up. It seemed we climbed for several hours, and of course we paused several times to rest. I was discouraged and believed we would go on climbing forever — but I told myself I only thought that because I was merely a child and children think such things. Finally we reached the top and, panting, stood looking down a hall.

The floors were ripped up, big hunks were tom from the ceiling and walls, doors were pulled off their hinges and lay scattered among the boards and piles of debris.

Father mumbled to himself, but then he and Mother went on and I hurried to keep up with them. Then as if they had found what they were looking for, we stopped before a door that was still intact. We stared at it as if it were a picture in a museum.

It was a large brown door and the knob was a gnome's head: bulging eyes, big nose, grinning mouth with the tip of its tongue sticking out. The knob was shiny from use, and I wasn't surprised — after all, hadn't we traveled all this way to find it? I felt reassured and was ashamed that when we were climbing the narrow stairs I had thought Mother and Father were making a big mistake.

Then Father reached for the knob. His hand traveled the distance to the knob with such slowness that I had plenty of time to think: I thought about my dog Spot and my cat Urbane who were home waiting for me, and I thought about Mother, how she was probably at this moment also thinking about the door and how slowly Father's hand was moving. I had plenty of time to think even beyond that, and I went clear to the frontiers of utter boredom as the hand moved for the knob.

It reached the knob and began turning it. It turned and turned. We waited. Then Father started opening the door.

Mother and I stepped back to allow plenty of room. Farther back — stumbling over debris. Farther back. With both hands Father forced the door wide open. There was a perfect closet. Even I recognized its perfection. Father nodded, turned to me, and with his right hand motioned to the closet.

I felt Mother's hand on my shoulder, not pushing, but communicating as explicitly as if she had touched her big lips to my ear and put the words into me. I stepped into the closet, turned, and looked out at them standing on a pile of debris, the cracked and ruined wall behind them ...

After Father shut the door, they stayed out there a long time, talking. Then they walked up and down the hall, stopped outside the closet, and talked again. There was a hush, and I knew Father had put his ear to the closet. "I'm still here, Father," I whispered.

They walked off and I knew they went down to the second floor, then down the other stairs to the first floor, then to the huge room where they probably stood looking at the fireplace, and then they went to the front door, waited a moment, thinking about ... I don't know. Maybe they had a conversation. Then they went out the door and shut it after them.

They have gone farther than our home. They have gone to another country. I am still here and will be until I can do something about this closet, the door, then the hall — all that debris, all the shattered walls and the ripped up floorboards, and then all the rooms on this floor and so on ... to downstairs. Last of all I'll have to do something about that fireplace. But until I do everything, I wait. I'm not waiting for someone to open the closet door. I would be foolish to be waiting for that — and, after all, I wasn't born yesterday.

FLOWERS IN YOUR HAIR

HE HEARS SOMEONE HUMMING THE SONG before he opens his eyes. The person murmurs, be sure to wear some flowers in your hair, and he is filled with contentment. He knows the song but he isn't sure where he is. For that matter, he isn't sure who he is, though this is normal, he tells himself. This happens to everyone at one time or another, perhaps to some more often than others. Eventually you will wake and in the first moment of waking not knowing who you are. A part of you is traded for a dream you were having, and then it evaporates right before your eyes.

Just those words, be sure to wear some flowers in your hair, and part of the tune, that's all he can remember. But it's enough. He vaguely decides he doesn't want to remember any more of it. For, once remembering begins, everything else will come back, his schedule of appointments for today, all the ordinary worries of an ordinary life, and the problems. All that can wait. There's plenty of time. Meanwhile, he will enjoy this feeling of being ... there, wherever it is.

"It's nice to just lie here and be free for a moment," he says out loud, though he only whispers it.

Someone says, "Yes."

He takes a deep breath and as he slowly releases it he feels he is floating, being lifted, and he can go either way now — sleep, or stay here in this warm glow, teetering between each breath as if he can choose to breathe or not breathe, a wonderful, peaceful feeling of being in complete control. "Sleep can wait," he says, and the person lying beside him says, "Yes." It occurs to him that the person lying beside him is his mother. He smiles at how ludicrous that is, while at the same time how tender and sad — though he doesn't know why and turns his mind away from it by turning his head the opposite way and opening his eyes.

The wall beside the bed is blank and unfamiliar.

"Tis so strange," he says, trying to speak louder in a normal firm tone, but it comes out as the same expectant whisper. And he doesn't listen to what the person lying beside him says, because he suspects it will be another Yes and he's already tired of this person.

Wake up in the morning, enjoy a few moments of blessed amnesia ... "Yes," the person lying beside him says. He remembers hearing someone say "... and you can enjoy a few moments of blessed amnesia before everything comes crashing down around your ears ..." Did he say that himself? He can almost see the face, the brave smile, or trying to be brave.

"Oh shut up," he says at exactly the same time the person lying beside him says, "Yes," and he waits through the next few seconds, expecting that now everything will rush back into place — his life, the people, his job, the whole world, the sky, the roofs of buildings outside his window ... The image of buildings outside a window almost holds, though the buildings he sees aren't familiar.

"So," he says. He takes another deep breath and holds it as long as he can, to get as much oxygen from it as possible, then lets it leak out of him. "Who am I, after all?" he whispers.

But he doesn't care. The moment has passed. As moments do. "Yes," the voice beside him says. And now he feels exhausted. Simply exhausted.

"I am dying, Egypt," he whispers and a memory rushes up as if to assist him, but just part of the memory: he sees a person upon a stage, a person he nearly recognizes.

Am I an actor? He keeps the thought inside himself because he doesn't want the person lying beside him on the narrow bed to hear, and also because he is too weak to speak aloud. Maybe I'm a singer.

He tries to see himself performing, and though he can't remember the face of that person who is himself, some of the words return and he hears be sure to wear some flowers in your hair ...

And more of the song, the magic of the tune and the words becoming stronger and bringing back the glowing mood of promise and love. Oh, yes, he remembers his heart pounding and the words of that old song going through his mind, in fact he had been humming it that day so long ago, though perhaps it was only yesterday, "If you're going to San Francisco, be sure to wear some flowers in your hair ..." when he arrived in the city.

Yes! That day comes back vividly! Every detail stands out with perfect distinctness. It is all beginning again. He reaches down and picks up his suitcase.

He has just got off the bus. He has just arrived in San Francisco. He is young and he is in love. He walks out of the bus station and, just as he had prayed for, he hasn't gone far before someone lets him look into his yes.

DAWN OF THE FLYING PIGS

THE SUMMER JIM AND BUZZY ROUGHNECKED, Jennifer went with them to the oil fields and sat in Jim's old station wagon reading by a kerosene lantern and eating raw turnips. She was pregnant with me and craved turnips. On their breaks Jim and Buzzy sprawled out in the back of the car and listened to the Cardinals' games on the radio while they ate their sandwiches. Then they slept until Rufus Troop blew his whistle, or they just lay there, too tired and depressed to talk, looking out at that big steel derrick lit up brighter than day and glaring like an altar of steel, and they thought about Sandra Goddard, Rowena Pribble, and all the trouble Jim had got them into showing off.

Thanks to Jim, that had been The Year of the Hard On at Mt. Vernon Township High School. Sandra Goddard and Rowena Pribble, the yearbook editors, just made it official by working a dozen good ones into Golden Memories and Sports Moments, airbrushing cars, school buses, buildings, hillsides, and the map of Illinois. If you turn the yearbook this way and that, you can find them lurking everywhere.

But the honors went to Jim. Sandra and Rowena succeeded in sneaking one of his into the yearbook. You can't see it at a glance, because there are so many people in the picture, a foldout with a hundred people crowded into the locker room; the Rams had just won the Christmas tournament — and like everyone in the crowd, you tend to gaze at the trophy the boys on the team hold over their heads.

Jim has an arm in the air, though he's so far from the trophy that, after you've spotted the erection and look again at his smile and the peculiar way he is standing, bent out from those around him, you suspect that he raised his hand to get your attention. Sandra and Rowena had doctored the photo, using certain Polaroid pictures which had floated around school that year. But Jim had been, indeed, the subject of those Polaroid pictures, and everyone recognized him, for by then he was very well known; that is, that part of him, which had become a legend in its own time, as they say.

Jim was expelled three weeks short of graduation — not just because of the yearbook but for everything else that year, for turning the school into a place haunted by hard ons and rumors of hard ons, for all the stunned fascination, the frenzy and adulation. (Sandra and Rowena graduated, went off to college, got married, etc.)

When Jim's mother protested (that's Rita, whom I called Grandma when I was a child), the principal told her that not graduating should be the least of Jim's worries. Twenty-odd daddies, uncles, and big brothers hoped to get their hands on him — and probably would, when the time was right.

Aside from those individuals, a lot of people, hundreds, wished that Jim would just vanish from the face of the earth. That is, go back to California.

But Jim couldn't go anywhere. Broke and desperate, Rita and Jim had loaded his three little sisters and all the clothes and dishes and other things they had room for into and onto their old station wagon and, breaking down every twenty or thirty miles and waiting for charity to get them going again, spent the summer of 1969 going from southern California to southern Illinois. That's another story.

They were true Californians and knew they were going the wrong way but they had no choice. They would have gone on welfare in California but Jim's father was crazy and had vowed to kill Rita and all the children. So they would live with Rita's half-blind old mother, Jim would finish his last year of high school, he would get a job.

But the boys and girls at Mt. Vernon Township High School had never seen anything like Jim. He was golden-haired and golden-skinned; he was tall and strong and good-looking, a great athlete, and one day after football practice someone had a radio in the locker room and on the way to the showers, with a towel around his waist, Jim started dancing, the towel fell off, he kept dancing, and he was doomed.

Jim did vanish, as so many people wished he would, but not back to California. Rufus Troop gave him and Buzzy jobs where no one could find Jim, out in the middle of nowhere.

Buzzy later became my father in a sense, though I've never called him that. He graduated but it didn't matter, he wasn't ready for anything, least of all so-called life. He would gladly have stayed in high school another year or two. On the basketball squad he had been good at guarding and dribbling, but he was too shy to take a shot. Buzzy is in the famous locker room picture, though he can't be seen. In Jennifer's yearbook (Buzzy and Jim threw theirs away) he showed me where he was "Right . . ." putting his finger on a space between two people, "there." With a magnifying glass I saw a white sliver which might be half of a face.

By August of that summer, Buzzy and Jennifer were Jim's last and only friends. But his showoff days were done, anyway. Everything was finished.

But nothing is ever finished. Time is layered. If you could live long enough and stand back far enough, you could probably even see stratifications. Jim didn't live long enough to see any stratifications, wouldn't have had any idea what I'm talking about. Though the night he got torn up pulling pipe he did learn the past is never finished with us.

An oil rig at night is spectacular in a glaring, outlandish way, with lights strung up on the derrick and around the edge of the drilling platform like footlights on a stage, though the only audience out there are the animals that come to take a look, and the woods itself which winds through the county like an endless snake. (All this is from what Jennifer told me. She planned to write a book about it, someday, lots of books about everything.)

The rig is encased in a tremendous shrill ringing shell of steel noise from an engine so powerful it can turn the drill a mile down in the earth. The men stuff cotton in their ears and tie bands around their heads with flaps over their ears under their hard hats to try keeping the noise out, but it's impossible, for they're immersed in the noise like fish in a bowl filled with mercury. The men yell back and forth just as if they can hear each other — it takes a long time to get used to the idea that there's no way you can be heard. Even after they start using hand signals they forget and yell at each other.

They have to pull pipe if they hit rock. The drilling stops and they pull all those long steel pipes out of the hole one by one and pile them by the platform. Finally, out comes the big old drillhead, the thing that has been down in that unimaginable place boring deeper and deeper. The drillhead that grinds through rock looks like a bunch of fists studded with steel triangles. The men put this drillhead on the first length of pipe, stick it in the hole, and lower it down until there's room for another length of pipe up in the derrick and screw it to the first pipe. This goes on and on until they have a mile of pipe in the hole and the drillhead is ready to gnaw through solid rock. After they grind through the rock they put the other drillhead on. Back and forth. Sometimes that summer Jim and Buzz would be exhausted from pulling pipe night after night. Other times they just drilled smoothly along.

When Jim got hurt they had been pulling pipe all night. It was about 4 a.m. Jennifer had been reading, then dozed off. She didn't like being out there with them, but she had a premonition, which she kept to herself, and she was afraid to stay alone at night in the dinky little house the three of them were living in that summer. When she woke up she got out to pee and give the mosquitoes a chance to bite her right where you almost never put repellant. She was watching them work, not really watching but seeing without thinking about it.

Jim was running out, as they call it. When a length of pipe was pulled out of the hole up into the derrick, Jim looped a heavy chain around an end of it. Sometimes he just gave it a sling. Then the man at the controls of the winch hit the gas, fiercely yanking the chain and spinning the pipe to disconnect it. Then Jim ran out — grabbed the down-end of the pipe and skated down a muddy steel ramp off the platform, swung the pipe onto the top of the big stack that had already been pulled out, and on a signal the top end was released and the pipe clanged down into place.

All this happened very fast. They would get a rhythm, especially the ones who were young, strong, natural athletes like Jim, all the operations and movements blurring smoothly into each other.

They had been doing the same thing for several nights — hitting rock, pulling the pipe, then going through the rock, pulling the pipe, then hitting rock again. To break the monotony they had raced to see who could pull and run out with the most pipe in an hour — Jim won. After that, they brought speakers out of their cars and had some music. Jennifer didn't know how they could hear, inside all that noise. From the station wagon, the music and the noise wavered in and out of each other. The men had started working along with the music, not exactly in time with it but doing a kind of whirling, sloppy dance, sometimes fast, then steadying out, then fast again. Sometimes the young guys would get caught up and go so fast and so hard that they wouldn't know until they stopped that it had emptied them out. Jennifer saw that Jim got caught up with doing that. Sweating hard and gleaming like a piece of machinery, the fool had stripped down to his shorts and boots.

And Jennifer knew the instant it started, felt the realization form in her mind at the same time if not maybe even sooner than the idea occurred to Jim: he took off his shorts. She groaned, said out loud, "Oh Jim you idiot," trying to pierce that gleaming steel case of night air and noise and the yellow tin hat he wore. If he heard her, a murmur at the back of his mind, he ignored her.

The men clapped and whistled, of course. They stood looking up at the drilling platform just as if they were watching a show in a roadhouse. Those roughnecks no doubt watched with much the same unfamiliar emotional reaction which the high school boys had felt, a mixture of awe, confoundment, and a surging belligerence, ending with the same furious or cold resentment which guaranteed for Jim an enemy in every man, except Buzzy, who saw how big he was and how proud of it he was. And it was quite a show, swinging and swaying up there on the drilling platform — he knew how to get the most out of it, he had practiced a lot, the two of them put on quite a performance.

When Jennifer told me this, here she closed her eyes. In grief and dread of what happened next. Though now, as I close my eyes, what happened is enhanced vividly. Inside all that incredible noise shines a steel cocoon of silence encasing the drilling platform. And I hear the same music I heard yesterday, almost miraculously, as I leaned back from the desk where I am writing this. I looked out the window of my room in the Hotel Tyrol in Madrid and heard, from down in the hotel kitchen, the Beach Boys singing I wish they all could be California girls — while Jim dances in the bright lights on the drilling platform, watching his hands automatically sling the chain around the pipe, then he spins on his heels and it happens.

The man operating the winch guns it half a second too soon. That's all it takes. The chain is loose, doesn't take bite on the pipe, and is yanked free of the pipe — the free end lashing straight out, and as Jim comes spinning the opposite direction something flies away out of the bright lights of the drilling platform, and as I close my eyes and see this I think of that custom

85

of leaving a little window open in the room where a person is dying so the spirit can leave on its long flight.

Now there is that awful silence which comes when something final and forever irreparable happens and everyone realizes it at the same time. Jennifer is rising from where she squats beside the car. Jim turns again, slowly, like that last slow lap after a race, and he is looking down at himself now, too — before, he would only glance down when he was showing off, letting everyone else do all the looking. But now he takes a long, breathless look at it, more breathlessly than anyone in the past.

Jennifer runs toward the drilling platform. Buzzy and the others start up the platform steps in that stunned, suspended way people approach calamity, as if it is a pit into which they might skid.

"My God, oh my God, what have you done?" Jennifer is yelling as she runs toward the platform. She tries to run up the muddy steel ramp and falls so hard she's afraid she has broken her chin, broken her left wrist, and killed the baby — me. No one notices she has fallen — they are all turned toward Jim — as Jennifer struggles up the ramp.

Jim is bent over, holding his hands between his legs. There is no blood. My God, how lucky, is Jennifer's first thought, how lucky, how lucky, how lucky. She is yelling but can't hear her own voice and the men on the drilling platform are talking too, she can see by the movement of their mouths, the veins standing out in their straining necks. He keeps turning away from the men as they try to see the front of him, until finally that isn't possible, he is surrounded, but he keeps turning anyway, then he sees Jennifer. His eyes are bulging, his lips are smashed flat against his teeth in an awful grimace unlike anything she had ever seen on his face or anyone's, his face is so rigidly flat the thought flashes through her mind that the chain struck his face, gouged out a part so cleanly his face can't bleed.

Then Jennifer saw what the men had no doubt already seen, blood dripping from between his fingers.

"Let me see," Jennifer yelled.

He turned away from her and she followed him in a circle, leaning forward and trying to take hold of his wrists. Another came up beside him, and one on the other side, holding him still, and Jennifer knelt down in front of him saying, "Let me see, you must let me see," and gripping his wrists she tried to pry his hands away from where they were cupped between his legs, which was impossible — all the men together couldn't have pulled his hands away.

Suddenly the big drill engine stopped, Rufus Troop had shut it off, which left only the generator, in contrast seeming to be barely a hum, and the radios which one of the men ran down to turn off, and when finally Jim let Jennifer take his bloody hands from between his legs, they saw at the same time, Jim looking down at himself and Jennifer kneeling between his knees, and the men crowding around to look, that the worst possible thing had happened. The chain had struck Jim just as he spun the opposite direction, shearing off the end of him.

"Oh Jesus," someone whispered. It hung straight down limp and headless. It looked like a finger drooling blood. Jim staggered and swayed forward, the men caught him and laid him down. Rufus Troop ran to the doghouse and got a first aid kit. They gave Jim a big wad of bandage to hold there and stop the bleeding.

Jennifer went down the steps of the drilling platform, wanting to run down them, to fly down them, but making herself go down them carefully, holding the rail. A pool of blackness ringed the ground close to the edge of the platform, the area shadowed from the lights on the derrick. Jennifer could see absolutely nothing — she couldn't even see the ground itself as she lowered a foot off the bottom step. Then she was afraid to move because she couldn't see anything.

She went along the platform until she was to the corner, then she cut out at an angle and, back in the light again, ran as hard as she could to the car. She grabbed the kerosene lantern and with her hands shaking so badly she could barely control them, she tore a match from the book and tried to strike it. The little head snapped off. She tried another, pinching the matchhead — it didn't strike but smushed across the striking surface. She struck match after match, then threw that matchbook away and dug in the glove compartment for another one.

Finally she got the lantern lit. She ran back to the edge of the platform and shading her eyes with one hand against the glare of lights on the derrick, she started searching the ground. Cigarette butts, matchsticks, cardboard cartons, candy bar wrappers, pop bottles and aluminum cans, ripped up paper bags, a whole loaf of bread with the end of the wrapper torn open maybe by animals and the slices fanned out like a hand of cards, and boards and broken pieces of equipment slung off the platform, thousands of crumpled and twisted things that Jennifer had to look at closely, even reaching down and picking things up and moving them slightly because what she was looking for might be hiding in the shadow of even the littlest thing. And she had to be very careful where she walked, looking twice carefully each time she took a step.

On the platform Jim wailed, sounding less like himself or any person than some animal that the men up there were torturing just to hear its desperate suffering and the words, "Oh my God, my God, my God," that came out as he gasped for breath.

Then she heard them tromping on the platform. They had picked him up and were going to carry him down to a car and start the long drive into Mt. Vernon. Running up the platform steps as they were bringing him down, she told them to wait, that she was going to find it, she had to find it. They just kept coming, making her back down, and she ran beside them, saying it over and over, and they just continued toward one of the cars.

She ran back to the place where she had been looking. She held the lantern closer to the ground, stooping down as if utterly fascinated by the dusty earth and all the pitiful rubbish.

They were putting him into the back seat of a car. Jennifer ran over to them and yelled at them to please, please wait. One of them looked at her, his eyes blank, his face as vacant as a cow's, as if the words Jennifer spoke with exaggerated, absurd slowness and distinctness were quite beyond his grasp. "Wait. Give me ... two minutes. That's all it will take. Two ..." putting her face right in his, "minutes."

"He's bleeding to death, goddamnit," one of them said. "There's not time to wait. We got to get him to the hospital."

Holding her hands over her head Jennifer screamed, "I'll stop the bleeding! I know how to stop the bleeding!"

This baffled them.

"I'm a nurse!" she screamed, amazed and thankful that she had popped out with that — for it worked! One of them even said, trancelike, his lips slowly moving as if these words were the first he had ever spoken, "A nurse."

"But first," she said, "I must find it."

Two of them nodded. They understood!

"And then I'll ..." She didn't finish because she had no idea what she would do. "Just wait. Wait. Don't take off. I'll go find it ... ," backing away, still holding up both hands.

"We'll come help you find it," one of them said.

"No! There's too great a risk of ... trampling. The light is bad. I have to look with this" — holding up the lantern — "and I have to look ... up close" — she held up her hand in front of her face — "like this. So just wait here. I'll find it in just a minute."

She backed away and they stared at her as if hypnotized, and as she went back to the side of the platform she looked several times over her shoulder.

Before she was into the center of the area where she thought it might be, she started searching, for she had really no idea where it might be except she had seen it flying in this general direction. As she bent down she realized that the area she intended to comb had gotten larger, and that the longer she searched, the more area she would have to include. A big spider going along stopped when it saw her and stood its ground.

The car started. "No!" she screamed. But she couldn't move from where she stood. If she ran to stop them, she was certain she would step on it, crush it, grind it into the earth.

They drove down toward the deep-rutted road and stopped by the generator. She heard shouting in the car, an argument that ended with one of them yelling at the top of his lungs that they couldn't leave the goddamned thing running with nobody the hell out here. One of them got out of the car and turned off the generator. The bright lights on the derrick went out. Jennifer stood in the lantern's dim circle.

The sense of urgency expanded all around her as in the darkness the woods came closer, came right up to her. She stopped searching, straightening with difficulty against the pain in her back. Holding the lantern high, she looked up at the derrick, hulking even larger in the dark ... and she realized that in combing the ground she had moved out too far from the platform, into the trampled and rutted grass.

She went back closer and pressing hard with her arm against the small of her back, leaned down again and resumed searching, worrying that where she was looking now was an area which she had already searched. "I need some kind of system" she said out loud. But maybe just once over wasn't good enough. All right. She started to get down on her hands and knees. Then she froze.

At the same time something moved through the black air above her head — how close she couldn't tell but she heard the soft muffled sound and felt the subtle stir of wind as it passed — she realized that something which she had passed over a minute ago was a strange object, some kind of strange bug or maybe a grape, but it didn't look like what she was searching for, didn't look like anything, really. And now she was certain she was standing on it.

Bending down as far as she could, so that she could see the space beside her right foot, she placed her foot there and looked at the flat grass where her foot had been. Nothing. She repeated the process with her left foot and sighed with relief that she hadn't been standing on it. Then she carefully turned and bending down as far as she could . . . she found the object again.

It bore no resemblance to what it was. It was just a little scrap, not even the complete piece of him that was torn off, though maybe it was, having yielded to that mystery of nature which everyone knows who has butchered or watched a butcher work, that all the parts and pieces, when they're cut and torn apart, make a sad little pile much smaller than their sum.

She drove as fast as the station wagon would run, the old thing wallowing over the road some farmer had made bringing equipment through the woods to a patch of fields. She felt the baby struggling around, quite disgruntled at all this. When she reached the gravel road, she floorboarded the gas and the car slowly gained speed until it was lumbering down the narrow road at a flat out 50 miles an hour.

She had driven about ten miles when she saw the other car stopped in the road and the men standing beside it with the doors open. She hit the brakes and the station wagon's rear end started coming around. She let off, blinked the headlights, and blaring the horn, passed as far as possible to the other side of the road without sliding off into the ditch. The men scrambled out of the way as she roared by.

She finally got it stopped and backed up, almost banging into the front of the other car. They just looked at her as she came up. "Well?" she said. "Well? What's wrong?"

Buzzy mumbled something, it sounded like he said He's dead. "What? What's that?" she said, her voice rising as she cut through them to the back door of the car where Buzzy stood, and he spoke again, low and confidential as if not wanting Jim to hear, "He's dead. He was drinking some whiskey and he just up and died."

She was speaking but she had no idea then or later what she said, maybe it was only a shrill eeeee which had started to be He is not dead but didn't get completely or even partway formed as she shoved Buzzy out of the way and moved into the back seat over Jim as he lay on his side with his legs drawn up. She couldn't listen for his breathing because she couldn't make herself be silent, hearing-far away herself saying over and over No no no no ... until he moved, she was certain he moved, a twitch in his shoulder.

"He's not dead," she announced for them outside the car and for Jim, too, inside that whiskey-smelling darkness in which he lay, the darkness seeming to emanate from him as he went farther and farther from her. She got out of the car. "Don't move him. Don't start the car. Wait right here" — though she already knew the car couldn't get around the station wagon.

In the station wagon she carefully moved the Tupper Ware box so that she could sit in front of the glove compartment. That night she had brought turnips in the box. Now it contained the little piece of him. She dug into the glove compartment, throwing out bottle caps one by one, a can opener, poptop rings, a Marlboro box, matchbooks, two pencil stubs, and finally, after everything was out, trolling with her fingernails she snagged a piece of thread, rolled it between her thumb and forefinger, and when she picked it up, the needle was still on the thread.

She brought the lantern with her and had one of them light it, then told one of them to go to the other side of the car and hold down Jim's shoulders and for another to lean down on his knees and hold him still. After having one of them scoot the front seat as far forward as possible, she squeezed into the back, kneeling on the floorboard and leaning over him.

He woke up, or it was more like coming back. The whiskey had already hit him pretty good, but he realized she was there, realized she was Jennifer, knew where he was more or less, and they talked to each other, their voices

91

high and strained, and he didn't understand what she meant when she told him what she planned to do, and when she leaned down and began, he lurched, bending double and closed on himself to protect himself from further pain.

She backed out of the car. They would have to get him out of there and hold him bent back over the hood of the car so she could get to him.

It took all four men to hold him still on the hood while Jennifer leaned down into his bloody groin, Buzzy holding the kerosene lantern in one hand while he lay on his side across Jim's chest, the lantern drawing the insects, curious at this spectacle, some even alighting on Jennifer s hands as she worked, a mosquito boring into her left wrist as she sewed the ragged little piece onto the ragged piece hanging out of him, the futility of it like a cloak of distance between Jennifer's mind and eyes, and the glinting needle and the pitiful black thread which she had used long, long ago it seemed, to sew a button on a dress, a button she had popped getting out of the car when she and Buzzy went to the grocery store one afternoon.

She didn't know how doctors went about lining up the jagged edges when they attempted the miracle of reattaching torn off parts. Just put the piece back on where it looks like it belongs and sew it on? Can you some-how line up all the tiny blood vessels? This won't work, she told herself.

It was futile. Worse than futile, it was preposterous. When word got out, when the idiots holding Jim down on the hood of the car told everyone they knew, and when all the people in Mt. Vernon and in high school knew, they all would crow with laughter. And the people who knew Jennifer, beginning with her mother, would gloat upon this peculiar and infinite compounding of her humiliation.

But now it didn't matter what people would say and how they would laugh, and how this part of Jim's legend would become a legend in its own right, and how his maimed condition would haunt him privately and pub-licly — she could just imagine the cruel jokes, about trying to drill for oil with his dick, and the dangers of dancing with his dick sticking out, and a thousand other things just unimaginable. As she worked, sweat beading on her upper lip, holding her breath each time she pushed the needle through his flesh, she thought ahead to how she would maybe tell me this, someday, wondered how she could if I was one of them, not someone who could hear the story and know how all the absurdity and terror were counterbalanced on the hood of that car in the middle of nowhere by determination and its mercifully blinding aureole of dignity. Or how at least in that hour the one who is caught up by necessity, forgetting herself in action, is blinded temporarily by knowing that this one thing, in this one moment, is not only the right thing to do but the only thing in the world that can be done.

Driving on into Mt. Vernon, Buzzy at the wheel of the station wagon — the rest of them following in the other car — Jennifer rode in the back with Jim, lying beside him to hold him still. He had drunk all the whiskey and had passed hysteria to babbling, talking to Buzzy and Jennifer, continuing to talk when they tried to answer. As the sun came up he loudly asked if Buzzy saw what he saw. "What's that, Jim?" Buzzy called back. "Pigs, man, don't you see 'em?"

Jennifer saw what he meant. The clouds in the east weren't just mounds turning from dark gray to purple to blazing pink, with some vague resemblance to pigs — they were indisputably and purely a herd of pigs driven up from the night and being launched one by one, wind on the horizon scattering them across the sky.

CHUMS

HE DIDN'T TRY TO ESCAPE but turned his back on the schoolyard, that wide, rolling prairie with clumps of brush and, far off, the brick maze where every morning we found things left the night before by roving gangs, strange, horrible things which were beyond our imaginations, though some of us, inspired by the strange needs of innocence, kept them and speculated on their uses, their meanings, with results that were invariably exciting, invariably terrifying.

The boys surrounded him, shoved him, tripped him, kicked him — he didn't try to defend himself. He was incredibly thin, a stick with a pale narrow face and sharp nose. I don't know why the gang had suddenly noticed him, why they singled him out. It's doubtful that he had done anything to provoke them, but the gangs that roamed the schoolyard and who in later years roamed the streets, occasionally returning nights to attack the school building for old time's sake and perform depravities in the brick maze — these gangs didn't require provocation. Straightforwardly vicious, they existed in a state of obliviousness: everything they did, every gesture, had a bland gracefulness, a stonelike superiority.

They got him down, took turns kicking him, then they stood him up and a boy on each side socked him back and forth good and fast — so fast his face blurred. The gang cheered, and I admit it outdid anything I had ever seen them do. The way his head twanged back and forth, faster and faster! — it was fascinating.

The cheering distracted one of the boys punching him; he broke the rhythm and the victim, propelled by the force of the last punch, stumbled to the edge of the tight circle, somehow through them ... and farther. He was running!

In disbelief we watched as he ran very slowly, barely lifting his legs, leaning forward very far as if that might make him go faster, and his running became a spectacle in itself. Stunned, the gang let him reach the school building and turn the corner.

"Come on," someone called, and they trotted to the building. The gang rounded the corner, came back, stood with their hands on their hips, looking at each other. Their fine little victim, the thin, narrow-faced boy, had disappeared. They even boosted someone up to look in a window, but he wasn't inside.

"We have not got him," one of them said and the others turned and looked at him as he said slowly and blankly again, "We have not got him." They walked off a ways and immediately forgot about the narrow-faced boy. Such a disappearance would keep me and the other secretive youths like me entertained, dazed, and content for weeks; we would be lost and tantalized in it, our parents would think we were sick or in love or in trouble with the cops. A disappearance would keep us going, for we loved the impossibility, we couldn't resist it; I would even go so far as to say we lived for it.

But the gang, of course, immediately forgot the victim had ever existed. They wandered off and soon they could be seen, far off, swarming across the prairie in running combat with another gang.

I went again to the corner of the building and stood with my nose to the corner, my left eye staring down the endless south wall of the building, and my right eye looking down the east wall. And I discovered the gang's victim was still there. In his extreme thinness he had become the corner, his narrow face and sharp nose becoming part of the sheer line of the corner. I stared into his eyes and whispered, "I see you.

The corner moved where his mouth was: "Don't tell."

"Yes. I'll tell them," I said. "Unless you give me something."

The corner closed as he closed his eyes and I could see the corner straining around him as he tried to disappear totally. But he couldn't. He opened his eyes. "All right," he said.

"What'll you give me?"

"I don't have anything. I'll let you hit me."

"Fuck that. I want something to show. Something I can think about."

"I'll show you my place."

"I don't want to see your place. I want something."

"It's not where I live. It's my special place."

"Is it a club?"

"It's better than that. Something is there. In it."

95

"What?"

The corner wobbled as he shook his head.

"Is it a gang?" I said.

"It's like a person," he whispered.

He had me. I asked more questions, but he wouldn't tell me anything more. I stood between the corner and the playground, and he emerged from the corner, though by now the gang was at least half a mile away, beyond the brick maze: clouds of dust rose above them, for they had apparently won the battle with the rival gang and were now stomping them.

He stood close to me, looking at me with his severe, narrow face. He expected me to ask how he had done that with the corner, but I refused to ask. He turned and started off. I followed, calling, "When?"

He went faster, and I ran to keep up. "When?" I yelled. "When, god-damn you?"

Now he was running across the playground as before, not moving his arms or shoulders but leaning rigidly forward from the waist, his legs not bending at the knees but stiffly swinging like scissors — but he was running very fast, and I realized he had earlier run slowly to deceive the fellows. He outran me easily. I stopped and as he topped a hill he called over his shoulder, "After school," and disappeared.

I spotted him after school in the crowd pouring from the building. He was hurrying, trying to lose himself among the other boys and girls. But I was right behind him. I reached out and grabbed his neck. I swung him around and smiled in his face. "Remember me?"

His eyes were enormous and yellow, with great wide whites. The yellow was unlike anything I had ever seen — yellow like a cat's, maybe, but deep and far like plains.

I turned away, angry, for he was grinning at me; he knew his eyes had surprised me. His grin took the corners of his mouth up sharply, making his mouth a quaint V under the V of his nose.

"I want to see that thing," I said.

"Sure," he said. "Let's go." I let go his neck and we walked on. "Nice day," he said. "My name is Bob. Where do you live? Do you have a dog?" He smiled slyly as we crossed a street. The crowd of children was thinning; in another block they had scattered completely; he and I were alone. "This way," he said, and we

96

turned down a street with few houses, and those the dark, run-down sort, some with boarded windows, maimed trees leaning into each other. Several blocks on, the street gave way to a dirt road, overgrown and untraveled.

"Do you live down here?" I said.

He jerked his hand, thumb up, over his shoulder: beyond empty fields with brush and thickets hulking larger and larger in the shadows of late afternoon, were hills, and beyond the hills a water tower hid in a clump of trees and low bushes. At the end of the road was a cemetery. He went up the path and under the iron arch that said Bethel in leafy iron letters. He looked back at me.

We followed a grass-covered lane through tombstones; statues of angels here and there looked off as if frozen stiff in the middle of doing something they started long ago. We topped a hill; the cemetery went on for miles, and I saw the first of the square stone houses. Not far ahead was a big one, a mausoleum as large as an apartment house, with barred windows set high in the walls, almost to the slate roof.

He turned off the lane and went straight to the mausoleum. He turned very slowly and smiled his V smile, his big yellow eyes looking right at me. "Here we are." Still looking at me, he reached out the other direction, took the handle of the big iron door, and it opened smoothly.

"It's in there," he said.

"What is?"

"The thing."

I shook my head.

"You can stand here and see it," he said. He stepped inside. I waited, then went to the door and looked into the long, empty room. Gray, distant light spilled down from the high windows. He stood half-way down the room, gripping the handle of one of the square steel doors that lined the walls. "Don't," I whispered, but he opened it, staring at me, and reached inside. There was a screech, then a grumble of rollers as he pulled out a casket — it was huge. And all the while he was looking at me, his face locked in that V grin, his eyes big.

I backed out and pulled the door almost closed, until there was a crack just wide enough for my face. I glanced behind me — there was nothing but the tombstones, the angels, the sky going away to night. I put my face to the crack in the door.

He lifted the casket lid, his head jerked my way and, grinning, he stepped up onto the side of the casket and unbuckled his belt and unzipped his pants. "Don't," I whispered. He grinned, dropped his pants. He didn't wear underwear. He put his arms out straight and swayed his hips. He kicked up his right foot, then his left, and clasping his hands behind his head, squatted down, his knees wide apart. Then he hopped down into the casket, reached down, and hooked big legs, bent at the knees, over the sides of the casket. He knelt, staring down seriously.

"What are you doing?" I whispered.

He ignored me.

I opened the door and tiptoed down the room. Just as I was about there, the legs slowly lifted straight up.

"Oh," I said and stood there.

After a while he stood and, hands on his hips, stepped up on the side of the casket again. The legs in the casket remained lifted in a big V, and he nodded toward them and said, "Want a turn with Rosie?"

I didn't answer.

He laughed and tumbled into the casket, banged down onto his knees, and lunged forward. "Uh," I heard.

The light dimmed, the walls dissolving. "What time is it?" he called over his shoulder. I looked at my Mickey Mouse and told him. He bounced around in the casket, then jumped up and the legs lowered. He climbed out, closed the casket, and pushed it on its rollers back into place and shut the steel door. "It's cold in here," he said, putting on his pants.

We carefully shut the mausoleum door, not banging it, and ran up the lane to the cemetery gate. At the road we cut across empty fields toward the water tower looming above the low houses. His house wasn't as bad as some of the others. He asked if I wanted to come in. I said no.

He waved and went in. I started off, then came back and looked in a window. He was in there with his family — a mother, a father, a sister and a little brother. They had joined hands and were dancing around the dinner table. I heard them laughing. Then he saw me looking in, and as he danced by he squinted his yellow eyes and stuck out his tongue.

Backing away, I turned to the darkness.

HEROES AND VILLAINS

MIRNA HEARD A CALLIOPE, the ripply booping like great blue bubbles floating up, and beneath her sleep mask she wondered if her daughter, Eileen, had at last revived from her trance, slipped out of the hospital, and brought this music home with her. But the calliope was so faint perhaps it was the soundtrack of a lingering dream in which cheetahs passed airily through a conversation Mirna was having with policemen. The cats looked over their shoulders with black, insouciant eyes, listened to Mirna and the police, then puckered their lips and precisely whispered the same word again and again — a word Mirna couldn't hear and which the police, ignoring the cats, missed. Mirna believed she could solve the mystery if she could only hear that word and pass it on to the right someone. The calliope faded and the dream slipped away.

Removing the mask she sat up and looked about, amazed to find she had slept in the large, high-ceilinged gallery. The walls were lined with old books which gasped and bowed when opened. Above the books badly foxed engravings hung among portraits of whiskered worthies from another century; according to the yellow velvet booklet which Mirna's son-in-law, Mickey Vozzio, acquired with all the pictures at an auction in Hollywood, one of these mutton-chopped notables was a descendant of the Sheriff of Nottingham! The picture which enjoyed prominence, though, was a huge and murky landscape by a fellow inspired and cursed by the conviction that his best work came to him late in the afternoon just as everything was sinking away. His hillsides, millstones and meadows, presumably immortalized, were as the painting faded into itself, suggesting things beyond what the artist could have found even in his finest fits of melancholy. Inevitably someone, maybe Mirna herself would someday stand before the picture and, after first seeing nothing but a vast brown and black rectangle, and after then penetrating her own dim reflection on the protective veneer, see at last movement, deep and vague — Gypsies slipping across the fields at night, the ponies' bells muffled, the wagons' wheels greased so the sheriff and his ruffian posse wouldn't hear. Or would she see profounder, more sinister doings? All enclosed by a wide gilt frame in which rampant cupids blasted clarions at the backs of each other's heads and sent doves surging determinedly through the molten sky and over the antlers of stags, tangled in the golden underbrush of cupid hair, on the trail to Sherwood Forest.

In a far corner was a large leather chair, Mickey's, though Mirna had seen him sit in it only once. (She had in fact seen her son-in-law that one time shortly before the police let her peek into a brown paper bag containing what she was told was Mickey Vozzio himself.) The walls in that corner were badged with breastplates, broadswords, battle-axes, spiked truncheons, and muskets — all plastic. Beside the chair a Duncan Phyfe table with Mickey's short-wave radio waited his return: here he would sit with a cigar and brandy, and get the results from Caliente, Del Mar, Hollywood Park, and tune in police calls from all over the world.

Morning had entered the house, proceeded from room to room and now stood in gray clumps and columns in the gallery like a tour of ghosts ready for the next spiel: "Here sat Mickey Vozzio on the fateful evening when a mysterious call beckoned him to affairs that ended with his untimely and incomprehensible death. In this recliner Mickey Vozzio's new wife, Eileen, sat knitting a sweater for her cat. While across from her, on the same sofa where just last night she struggled through the crowded, churning, rackety sleep which poets suffer nearly every night, sat Mirna Pooley, the Mirna Pooley, known here and there as the author of such volumes as *The Bawds of Baffledom; Oh Sweet Mystic Halloweenist;* and *The Albatross and Other Heavenly Birds,* herself a tourist of sorts, bon vivant, sometimes lecturer, but currently full-time grieving mother-in-law and worried mother of a terrifically sick daughter. That evening, just before the phone rang, Ms. Pooley looked up from the book on her lap and with that gaze easily mistaken for the foggy mood which verse evokes in gentler readers, she wondered if Mickey could use the excellent tax write-off of publishing a poetry magazine

Mirna sat up and tried a quick fantasy: Eileen and Mickey were upstairs in the master bedroom and all the rest was a bad dream ...

But she knew she was alone. Last night returned on great black wings. Mirna saw herself roaming through the house. She was looking for something, and though she found a great deal of everything, she couldn't decide what was a valid clue and what wasn't. All this was of course quite new to her, especially the telephone calls.

The phones kept ringing and she had answered them in this room and that as if she were hearing one by one from a chorus. With her notebook in hand, Mirna at first tried to take messages; she would give them to Eileen when she left the hospital. But her notes were too bizarre to pass on, though they might someday provide a poem of two. The phone calls were vortexes into which Mirna sank deeper moment by moment, the callers talking with speedy incoherence and a desperation which Mirna recognized though she understood nothing of what they were talking about. They talked on even when she tried to interrupt, their words racing faster as Mirna softly repeated, "Good-bye for now. Good-bye ..." and lowered the phone to its cradle There were several calls in a foreign language, but not Italian. Listening dutifully to the deep-voiced fellow, Mirna tried to feel through the totally alien words to the basic human hiding, she trusted, beneath it all. But she could make absolutely nothing of it, and after several of these calls it occurred to her that the fellow was merely gabbling. When he called again Mirna launched into it with him, coming forth with wild nonsense at which she discovered she was quite fluent and in which, she further discovered, she had a great deal to say. When the fellow hung up on her, she stood waiting for him to call back and was rather disappointed he didn't. Mirna had continued roaming through the house, waiting for a phone to ring, but none did. She at last picked up the receiver of one and found the line was dead.

She had started upstairs to bed when there was a knock. And the man at the door — Mirna was fairly sure this wasn't a dream, though now in the gray gallery it all seemed tremendously far away — was he a taxi driver? He wore shabby khakis too big for him and a billed cap with a badge. Maybe he was a Mexican policeman. As Mirna expected, she couldn't understand what he said, though it sounded vaguely English. She was distracted in part from understanding him by his remarkable face, yellow and protuberant as if his head had been squeezed from behind, bulging his eyes, jutting his lips, and creating at least a fistful of nose. She let him talk a while and then slowly shut the door in his face and went into the gallery, dragging behind her a polar bearskin under which she snuggled on a sofa. Just as she was slipping away, the thought floated through that the man, though unusual, apparently knew Mickey, was perhaps even his friend, for people do befriend taxi drivers and Mexican policemen, and then Mirna realized that while listening to the man she had noticed out the corner of her eye, without actually seeing, that his pants were unzipped. Were they really? Yes, she was certain. Perhaps he had been asking to use Mickey's bathroom.

Tinkling cheers, delicate with distance and the ambiance of dawn, came through the sound and bulletproof gallery windows. She went to a window, the bearskin around her shoulders.

The sloping lawn sparkled with dew. Large trees stood about, involved in that long and dour confabulation of trees. Around the lawn a fifteen-foot hedge concealed a fence, which Eileen had said carried enough juice to roast all the rhinos in the L.A. zoo.

Cavorting on the lawn was a troupe of small, nearly naked people. Mirna smiled, blinked several times, and decided they were actual people, though they were quite successfully coming across as elves, limberly cartwheeling, bobbing, and tossing each other about. They sprang off a blue trampoline and sailed blithely through the air, arms tight to their sides — to be caught at the last moment. They spun each other into somersaults and flips that zipped them across the wet grass like water bugs skimming a pond. To the side stood a red wagon with two white ponies in the traces; in the wagon was a calliope, and at the keyboard, with his legs crossed and buffing his fingernails, sat a little man in jockey boots, cap, and silks. When the tumblers saw Mirna, they gave a cheer, formed a circle, and did a frisking, lissome dance, glancing toward the window, their black eyes glinting with that sure slyness of persons who have already gone too far but intend to go even farther. A young man, naked except for a G-string shiny with dew, came up the lawn, his lips flared back from a large mouth of exceedingly white teeth, many more than most people have, his long blond hair flaming from his head as he ran. Under the window he flung open his arms and addressed Mirna. But Mirna heard only a cottony muffle of words — and, dimly, the calliope as it started up. Under the window the young man grimaced in a dramatic agony, his neck bulging. Mirna tried lipreading him. It seemed he was singing the same words over and over.

Mirna wondered if the young man and the rest had heard the news about Mickey. She smiled, then said silently but exaggeratedly, enunciating as though speaking underwater Mickey is gone. The young man stopped swaying and gesturing; the frenzy knotting of his face vanished. What? If only Mirna had a sheet of paper, but she had misplaced her notebook. With a finger she wrote the message on air, realizing as she did that to the young man it was of course written backwards: he frowned; Mirna shrugged. "Good-bye," she said and backed away from the window.

She went to the gallery door and peered down the dark hall. A suit of armor lurked half-sunk in shadows, the slits in the smug beaklike visor staring at the opposite wall while at the same time leering sidelong at Mirna. The mesh fingers of the right hand seemed to curl tighter around the grip of the mace they held.

Mirna hurried by the armor, through a door, and down a narrow passage. She entered the kitchen just as Pusser Boy was coming in by another door. Seeing her, he stopped and backed out. "Well," Mirna said. "Could it be someone wants his breakfast?" She went to the refrigerator and got her yogurt from the top shelf. The other shelves were filled with baggies of kidney. While she was peeling one open, Pusser Boy looked around the corner and slipped into the kitchen. He rubbed against the backs of her legs, then stepped inside the bearskin with her and stood with his tail between her thighs. She put the kidney down for him and, climbing onto a stool with her yogurt, watched him eat. Twice he paused, licking his lips and staring at her.

When they finished, Mirna waited as Pusser Boy paid a visit to his box in the utility room. Then she went down the hall to the staircase, looking back and seeing Pusser Boy was following but at a distance, stopping when she stopped. Upstairs he followed her down the hall to the master bedroom.

A purple arm stuck from under the closet door. Mirna opened the door: a tuxedo wadded on the floor shimmered silkily within itself like a fermenting jellyfish, and the closet had the fecund, rather rotten odor of the sea. On the racks leather jackets, vests, shirts and slacks, that appeared hacked from wood, hung among dresses, full-length gowns, and a dozen or so dungaree jackets stitched with big black apples, yellow-green sun bursts, tarantulas with baby faces, and, covering the back of one denim jacket, a maroon rubber vulva drooling candlewax into the motto Pussy Power. Mirna again searched pockets, finding rainbow condoms and toothpicks, pop-top rings and worry beads, hairpins and nine- millimeter bullets, lire, pounds, pesos, dollars, cents, and several grand in play money, and a hard as rock, mustarded, ketchuped and relished hotdog bun sans wienie.

Mirna put the clothes away and shut the closet door, convinced she had again let the clue she needed slip through her fingers.

She went to the cluttered dressing table where Jacqueline Onassis smiled from the cover of a movie magazine, her eyes large and oddly blank. On the front of a detective magazine the gray sky covered a shirtless, thin-chested boy being dragged through a ditch by large men in slickers and cowboy hats. On another, Charlie Starkweather and Caril Fugate sheepishly looked out at the world. There were racing forms with bilingual scribbles, lace bikinis, a fifty-dollar bill folded into a dense square and bound with a rubber band (Mirna refolded the bill and looped the band around it again) and a pair of white silk boxer shorts monogrammed with a lavender V looping and swirling like a pretty worm wriggling into flight. Jewelry boxes tried to outdo each other before an audience of coffee cups which, gaping with awe, revealed thick black residues caked in their bottoms. Mirna opened a box of chocolate-covered cherries and found among the crinkly wrappers a cigar butt, a jack of spades, and a Richard Nixon wrist watch. She replaced the lid and put the box on a rubber glove pointing to the tip of a lipstick poking out from a folded racing form. Mirna picked up a pair of yellow plastic opera glasses which, she had discovered the first time she looked into them, didn't give her a better view of things but showed her a tangle of two women, a man, and an object nearly as large as a fourth party which surely wasn't what it seemed to be, though now as Mirna took another look into the glasses (for even in there she might find the clue) she acknowledged that the object was indeed that.

In a drawer she found Eileen's big jar of pills with a masking-tape label penciled with an unending indecipherable sentence winding through itself and covering every square centimeter with words. Mirna unscrewed the lid and again was surprised by a familiar nose-tingling smell. This time she stirred around in the jar and uncovered a great white pill. She got it out, sniffed it — a moth ball. She dropped it and Pusser Boy trotted over and, as Mirna dug out a pill, a blue one big as a thumb and soft and wrinkled, Pusser Boy swatted the moth ball under the dressing table.

When Mirna returned from the bathroom, Pusser Boy let himself be picked up and carried to the bed. He lay stretched down her side, not purring, and though cheek to cheek with Mirna, Pusser Boy's amber eyes were sternly averted — not to the door but the wall as if he knew that when trouble comes it doesn't saunter through the door or pop through windows, but bulges out of walls.

Mirna hummed as thick blue welled up and she murmured in Pusser Boy's ear, "Oh silly goose, what shall we do, stick it down with paste and glue?" which wasn't exactly what she meant but as she tried to hear it again, the minnows flitted away and, leaning out too far after them, she glided onto the lake and lost herself.

That afternoon Mirna dressed in a rush and ran from the house. When she arrived at the hospital she was informed by Nurse Hudlow — an exceptionally tall person with a tendency to roll her eyes up, perhaps from habitually ducking doorways and checking the whereabouts of ceilings — that a group had tried to visit Mrs. Vozzio that morning. But Hudlow and the other nurses, who at that moment stepped from a room behind the nursing station, two powerhouses with oversized plastic tags on their uniforms announcing Spaag and Muldoon, had thrown them out: visiting hours weren't until one-thirty.

"Were they tumblers?" Mirna said, imagining that morning's troupe of little people tumbling down the corridor, the white ponies' hooves clattering, the calliope sending its hopeful tootle echoing through the hospital.

"Tumblers?" Hudlow said. "Ah — " rolling her eyes up — "no. More like actors. Actors being ordinary in gray suits. Ah — actors in politics, dicks and goons."

"Some of Mickey's friends, perhaps," Mirna said. The nurses walked down the hall with her. "Is Eileen resting well?"

"She — ah — remains catatonic."

Spaag leaned to Mirna. "That's resting very well."

They reached Eileen's room, all white except for furry shadows gathered in the corners and under the bed. Mirna entered and, stepping onto a stool, leaned over the guardrail and kissed Eileen. The smooth eyelids didn't flicker.

Turning, Mirna saw a young woman, a girl actually, no more than twenty years old, behind the door, squeezed in a corner beside a cart of blankets and rubber hot water bottles. The girl put her finger to her lips.

Mirna smiled at Hudlow, Spaag and Muldoon, shoulder to shoulder in the hall, and said, "Thank you so much for all you've done." The three moved off.

"What ... ?" Mirna started but the girl shook her head, her finger still to her lips. Her face was gray and thin, with the wistfulness of an ascetic waiting for the moment that would spring her into being someone else, or something else, or let her vanish altogether — and Mirna realized the girl bore a disturbing resemblance to Eileen! Did the hospital substitute dejected look-alikes for patients who were beyond fixing? But maybe the girl's vagueness had nothing to do with Eileen. Had this girl been irreparably shamed? Had she just recently and barely survived an onslaught of love fought with strange acts? Had she on a dare given herself to a giant? Or was she the sister of louts who gorged on pails of oatmeal, guzzled honey, then dragged her to the basement for a rampage? She wore a brown sack with Idaho Spuds arching a dark figure in a field. Her legs were long and bony, and ended in big gray feet. She wore gold rings on her toes. What mysteries we are, Mirna thought, and with a smile whispered, "Hello, my darling."

The girl made an indistinct sound-sigh, groan, or grunt — and, turning to the cart beside her, tucked in the blanket.

Going nearer, Mirna saw a yellow rubber water bottle at the end of the cart; the blanket's lumpiness suggested there were more. Then Mirna realized the blanket covered a person, soft and slick, the vague nose, mouth, and closed eyelids floating on the flat yellow face. "Oh my," she said.

"They cut him in half," the girl whispered.

"He must have been terribly sick."

"Huh?"

"I mean, for the doctors to perform such drastic ...

"It wasn't the docs. It was them." Mirna looked into her half-closed eyes, purple-gray, remote. "I guess you know they got the husband of that one." The girl nodded toward Eileen on the bed. "Crunched him down to a bouillon cube. But my Robert they sliced off half of him — the back half, from the head straight down. If he ever walks again he'll have to tiptoe everywhere — no heels." With a Kleenex she dabbed the yellow lumps which were Robert's eyes. "Do you have a cigarette?" she asked Mirna.

"I think …" She dug into her purse — or rather it was Eileen's purse she was carrying.

The girl lit a cigarette and blew a cloud of smoke toward the ceiling. "Sorry I brought Robert in here. I mean it's her room. But I gotta keep moving him around. If they get their hands on him again, I don't know what they'll do. Slice off some more. Or do it to me?" She stared off. "I wish I hadn't thought of that, because now they'll think of it too. And they'll cut me in half and make movies of Robert and me tiptoeing down the street. They have a big sense of humor."

"You know these people?" Mirna said.

"Sure I know them. Like the back of my hand. Everybody knows them. It's no secret anymore."

"I'm glad I found you," Mirna said and touched the girl's cold cheek, "for I am gathering material on the death of Mickey Vozzio and the mysterious shock that has driven her" – nodding toward Eileen - "into this deep sleep. You're certain the same people are involved in Mickey's death and" — she glanced at Robert.

"Who else?" The girl limped across the room and got an ashtray. Coming back, her hand on her side, she said, "I got a game hip. Say, I don't guess you could spare some change, could you?"

Mirna gave her some quarters, dimes, and pennies. The girl quickly counted the money and stashed it in a leather pouch hanging around her neck. She rubbed her hip and suavely said, "I'm a little stiff from balling." She leaned against the wall and, slowly scooting down, sat on the floor, her thighs against her chest. She pulled the sack over her knees and down to her ankles. "So you want some information. Are you a detective?" Mirna said she wasn't. "Okay. Just an interested party. So. The first thing you gotta learn is information without proof is nothing. You need evidence."

"Where can I get it?"

"Don't worry. I can give you all the evidence you will ever need. Enough for you and a dozen interested parties. I'll fix you up with Mr. Stein. Soon as I finish this we'll take off." She inhaled on the cigarette. She stretched out her long thin legs and rubbed her hip. She breathed out the smoke. "I think my lip has inflamed membranes. Look. " She pulled down her lower lip. "Touch," she said and, taking Mirna's thumb, ran it across the slick rim. "Uh? Do you have membrane problems?"

"No," Mirna said.

"You're lucky. Sit down." She patted the floor.

Mirna sat, her legs tucked under her, her skirt (or rather it was Eileen's) hiking up. The girl put her cigarette in the ashtray and, reaching right up, touched Mirna's mouth. Her hand smelled of smoke and metal. "I," Mirna started and the girl slipped a finger inside. She felt along the lower lip, then the finger slid in deep, along Mirna's jaw, turning and probing while the girl and Mirna stared intently at each other. "Nice," the girl said. "Real nice." She reached down with her free hand, took another puff on the cigarette, and ground it out in the ashtray. Then the finger came out of Mirna's mouth with a soft plop and swiftly, like a fish leaping from a pool directly into one's eye, slid up between Mirna's legs. "Please," the girl whispered. "I'm all alone now."

Mirna clamped her thighs together, stopping the hand.

"I'll help," Mirna said.

"Good." The hand squirmed.

"But."

"You draw the line on that?"

"I don't draw lines. But I want material and evidence."

"Okay. But you must pay the piper, and that's me." She leaned slowly forward, her eyes closing on their purple-gray crowd of villains, giants, wolves ... and Mirna licked her so blue lips and narrow tongue.

Pusser Boy was licking Mirna's lips or rather Mirna and Pusser Boy were tapping tongues as if trying to put his back where it belonged. Mirna removed her mask, and Pusser Boy jumped off the bed and from the room. Then far off, as if from a hollow wooden planet Mirna heard someone knocking. She put on one of Eileen's gowns and hurried downstairs. Looking out the tiny glass peephole in the front door, she saw the world not as a convex night, sleek and bulging, but a soupy, gray convex day. But she saw no one. She opened the door a crack. "Hello?" she whispered. Pusser Boy pushed his way out and slipped into the bushes.

Mirna shut the door and went from room to room looking out. From a rear window of the east wing she saw a large man who looked like Oscar Wilde sitting in a lounge chair by the pool. He wore a green velvet sports coat, pearl gray slacks, and white patent leather shoes with gold buckles. Before him a tall youth with spriggy red hair was stripping. Mirna believed she had seen the youth before. Down to his shorts, he bounded to the edge of the pool and, sticking in his foot, stirred a hole in the moss. He grinned at the man in the lounge chair, and now Mirna was quite sure she recognized the boy — that wide square mouth like a slot where one might sock in a cassette, and all those big teeth: he was the large-mouthed lad with flaming blond hair who had performed on the lawn with the tumblers! He dived into the hole.

His head popped up in the middle of the pool. He laughed and shook back his moss-streaked hair. It's cold. It's green, Mirna lipread as he called to his friend. He climbed out and with a whoop ran down to the far end of the pool. He bounced on the diving board, his arms lifted. Look. Look. His companion waved a large, long-fingered hand, and the boy dived in.

And the thick carpet of moss remained unbroken beyond the time he should have come up. Maybe it was so thick at the deep end he couldn't break through: Mirna pictured him suspended in blackness, butting his head against something like the sky.

His companion lit a cigarette and leaned back his head, large and shaggy, with black curls hanging down to tease his cheeks and nearly conceal his long ears. He closed his dark-ringed puffy eyes, and on his face settled a bloated serenity that was disturbed only by an occasional quiver of the chin and a petulance of the lips.

Mirna cranked open the window. "Yoo hoo!" He opened his eyes. "What happened to your young man?"

His forehead creased, his lips pursed with a pensive, weary irony, and he stared at Mirna. She felt he was seeing quite all of her. "Should I send for an ambulance?" Mirna said. "A doctor? The police?"

"No need." His voice was as effortless as a cloud. "I am the police."

He took a book from his pocket — Mirna's first slim volume! A collection she shared with the McCoy sisters, Beryl and Ida, with whom she skipped arm in arm, nude and gauzy, on the cover as if to refute the title,

We Wiser Disguisers. "Is it true that you are Mirna Mina Pooley?" he said. She affirmed she was. He rose slowly and with difficulty. He slipped the book into his pocket and, his heels clicking on the patio, walked to the window. Looking up, he said, "Well, are you going to unlock the door, or let down your hair?"

Mirna hurried to the nearest door. When she opened it, he was waiting, even larger than he seemed before, and there beside him, moss-smeared and dripping wet, was his sidekick, who wasn't at all a boy but a wiry thirty-year-old man standing with his clothes wadded in a ball. "Hi," he said and Mirna saw within the slope of his forehead, in his perfectly round gray eyes and gaping square mouth, an awful resemblance in the two men, as if they were grotesques of each other.

The gentleman in the green velvet sports coat spoke.

I am Basil Stein. I am inquiring into the death of Marvin Foster, a.k.a. Michael Fogstar, Mick Fallo, Mickey Nozzolio, Mickey Vozzio."

"He was Mickey Vozzio to me. Please come in." She showed them to the gallery where Basil Stein lowered himself onto a sofa and crossed his trunk-like legs. His companion stuffed his clothes in a vase and went about the room opening drawers and digging under the cushions of chairs and sofas. He found a stick of chewing gum which he unwrapped and stuck in his mouth — then he found some change. Laughing loudly, he brought it to Basil Stein who slipped the coins into his coat pocket.

Mirna said, "I was afraid he had drowned in the pool."

Basil Stein closed his eyes and slowly shook his head. "Roy can hold his breath for ten minutes, perhaps longer. Anyway, he found a room under the diving board." He opened his eyes and looked at Mirna. "Were you aware there is a secret room under the pool?"

"No. What is in it?"

Roy, on his hands and knees with an arm stuck to the elbow in the bowels of a sofa, said over his shoulder, "Nobody was home. It's just a little place with a little door."

Basil Stein took out *We Wiser Disguisers*, read a line or two, then looked up. "Why are you interfering in these affairs, my dear?"

"I happened to be in the country to see my publisher. A wire was waiting for me there from my daughter informing me she had gotten married.

I left New York immediately and arrived here in time to say hello to my son-in-law, see him off to his death, and put my daughter in the hospital. Now I am doing what I can to get to the bottom of it all."

"Then you're willing to cooperate with us in every way imaginable?"

"Yes."

"Hmm. Good. But need I point out that you're hardly adept? For instance, we were here earlier, spying, and you didn't know."

"It's true that it didn't occur to me that you were spying that morning. But I did recognize him" — nodding toward Roy. "Were you out there too?"

Basil Stein looked away aloofly. "In the calliope. But I have more important matters." He took out a notebook, glanced into it, put it away. "Have you ever been Mirna Cooney or Irene Rommel?"

"No. I have always been myself."

"You've never disguised, done a poem or two under a nom de plume, or chanced an afternoon as someone else?"

"Well ...."

"Okay." Covering his eyes with one hand, he held up the other as if he didn't want to know. He patted the cushion beside him and looked out from between his fingers. Mirna sat beside him. "We shall wait," he said. Reaching his long fingers into his hair, he began scratching his head. He closed his heavy-lidded eyes; the movement of the hand, hidden to the wrist in his hair, slowed, then ceased. Mirna believed he had fallen asleep. Then he spoke, but barely louder than a whisper. "Mickey's death was a shock to us all. In truth, I find it quite impossible to accept that he is really dead."

"I barely knew him," Mirna said. "I have tried to piece together his life with my daughter so that I might understand why she ..."

Basil Stein began speaking while Mirna was talking; she trailed off and listened.

"... and even earlier, I knew him as a child, we were school chums, following each other about the schoolyard, in the winter waiting around the corners for each other in the dark hallways and in the basement under the gymnasium. We laid traps for each other." Basil Stein chuckled. "His were always best. Such as the time he and his gang caught me in the storage room above the auditorium. They nailed me to the floor and wrote their names on me with burning sticks, and drew arrows and hands and naked women.

111

Mickey was on the chess team and the night he won the state championship, I caught his sister and made her eat stuff and she was in the hospital for a month. On graduation day, Mickey and I swore to be enemies to the end. We wanted to choke each other to death right there in the middle of the football field, but of course they wouldn't let us. I went to the Korean War and was a hero, while Mickey stayed home and made three million dollars in hot cars, whores, and smack. When we won the war, I came back and sneaked into his house — not this one but the one in Trenton — and sprayed kerosene everywhere, and I was there waiting when Mickey came home. I shot him in the stomach, but just once and with a twenty- two caliber so he would live."

Basil Stein sighed and, opening his eyes, looked around the room. "But that was years ago." He smoothed down his hair and sat up. "Nice place he has here. I like the art work. Especially that big piece with all the niggers hiding in it." He crossed the room and stood before the dark landscape. "I wonder what they're doing in there."

Roy, who had joined him, cupped his hand to Basil Stein's ear and whispered, rolling his big gray eyes at Mirna.

"Hmm," Basil Stein said. He turned from the painting. "Anything to eat around here?"

"Yogurt. And Pusser Boy's kidney."

"He's the cat, right?" Mirna confirmed this. "I find it strange that Mickey would leave his cat behind, to fend for itself and to ultimately starve." He took out his notebook and a pencil. "Cat ... still ... living," he said and dotted a period with a jab. "Okay." He yawned widely, causing Roy to yawn. "Give me the yogurt and what's-his-name's kidney."

When Mirna returned from the kitchen with a tray of food, thirty large men were wandering in the hall and milling about the gallery. They looked at her out the corners of their eyes and ignored her when she said hello.

Basil Stein ate the yogurt with a tablespoon. "I love it. This stuff is so good," he told her, looking up with his large dark eyes. But he had her throw out the kidney which he claimed was tainted. He said the pissy smell alone would make anyone sick.

Basil Stein and his men tuned in Mickey's short-wave and got the results from Hollywood Park. Between races they picked up signals from abroad, listening a while to a man distressed in the Indian Ocean.

For supper Basil Stein sent out for Chinese, and afterwards had Mirna sit with him and the others in the dark gallery. The curtains were open, and two or three men stood at each window, cranked open wide, with rifles and machine guns; the rest sat in chairs and sofas, and some sat on the floor, whispering. Around nine o'clock they heard the thrumming of a diesel: a huge fire engine with its lights off sat in the driveway. The driver switched it off and Basil Stein and his men squeezed the truck through the narrow space between the swimming pool and the house, and pushed it down the lawn to the trees. By the light of the moon they camouflaged it with branches and rose bushes. When they finished, the fire truck looked like a great pyre ready to be lit. As they went back into the house, Basil Stein slipped his arm around Mirna's waist. "We might need it," he said. "If not tonight, tomorrow for sure,"

Back in the gallery Basil Stein ordered a movie projector to be set up, and they watched jerky silent movies, grainy black and white, from Mickey's film library. Mirna recognized some downtown streets and buildings: there was the public library with Basil Stein himself trudging up the endless steps with an armload of books and nodding to the uniformed guard who opened the door for him. Basil Stein went in — and in a moment came out, crouching, gun in hand, grinning Roy's huge square grin. He jabbed the gun in the guard's back and sent him tumbling down the steps. There was the hospital: inside to the lobby where row on row of black people slumped against each other; then down a corridor to the door of Eileen's room. The door opened a crack and Basil Stein looked out at the camera and silently said, Leave me alone. In the ensuing fracas Basil Stein, Roy, and several other men were knocked about and thrown out by the nurses. More street scenes. A young woman in a short dress was yanked in a delivery truck by a large hook. An extraordinarily thin, literally flat, man and woman came tiptoeing down the sidewalk.

Several times Basil Stein told the projectionist to run something by again: the men roared when a huge truck spat a patrolman from its grille onto a wobbly motorcycle which straightened itself by bumping a curb and then zipped backwards down the street. Later, a dozen policemen sprang from a pile on the sidewalk and allowed a little person wearing a ski mask, with a round awed mouth, to pop up and back briskly into a bank.

Basil Stein sent out for sandwiches, and the projectionist showed color movies. The men came down from the roof and up from the basement and from their posts at the windows, and drank milk with their sandwiches and watched movies of naked people playing croquet, oiling each other, doing the twist, frug, and bunny hug, and rolling around with ponies and dogs. Basil Stein's men laughed, groaned, whistled softly. Then Mickey Vozzio, wearing the same purple tuxedo which lay on the floor of the master bedroom closet, bowed to the camera and welcomed them to the very room where they were sitting: it was filled with as many men and women as there were now policemen, but in the movie everyone was naked, gold, and sported glass phalluses.

Basil Stein and Mirna went up to the master bedroom and sorted through the things in the closet and drawers. On Basil Stein's suggestion Mirna tried on a pair of jeans and a red tank top. "Good," Basil Stein said. "Excellent." Next he picked the denim jacket with the big maroon vulva on the back. She put it on and walked about as Basil Stein lay on the bed, his hands clasped under his head. "But you need a wig," he said She tried one. "No. A long black one? Ahhh." He smiled, his eyes nearly closed. "Come here." He unzipped his fly, reached in, and pulled out a snubbednosed revolver. "Here, Patty," he whispered. "Don't let the schmucks take you alive."

They ate breakfast at Denny's. Then drove across town in a caravan of twenty patrol cars with red lights flashing, the fire truck bringing up the rear. Mirna rode in the lead car with Basil Stein. Roy, who had donned some of Eileen's clothes and an orange afro, rode in the backseat.

Basil Stein listened to dispatches, then switched to a rock station on a.m. He checked his watch, then nudged Mirna. "Get this." The disk jockey cut off the Beach Boys and announced that Patty Hearst and other members of the Symbionese Liberation Army had been seen leaving a local restaurant, and police were tightening a ring around them.

They were driving down a street of bare yellow houses. Black people looked out the windows as they passed and their front doors slowly closed. Basil Stein pulled off and stopped at the end of an alley. One other patrol car stopped, and the others went on.

Mirna got out with Basil Stein and Roy, and with the patrolmen from the other car, they walked up the alley to a house with a low stone wall. "This is it," Basil Stein said and the patrolmen went in the back door.

A woman yelled, a pan clattered and a chair was knocked over. The woman said loudly, "What you ... ?"

Mirna and Roy followed Basil Stein in. The patrolmen were handcuffing a black woman to an old washing machine. Two black men came in from the next room, their eyes big. "Down," Basil Stein said and pointed to the linoleum floor. The men lay down. Basil Stein, Mirna, and Roy stepped over them and went in.

The walls of the small dining room and living room were covered with framed photographs of black people standing in front of their homes with their cars, arm in arm at reunions in the park with tables covered with hampers and big bowls of food. There were pictures of black people with their children, with their dogs and cats, black soldiers grinning in Germany and Japan, and there was a picture of a stern old man with his mule. Football and basketball teams of bright-eyed boys stared confidently at Basil Stein. Everywhere there were big happy girls — girls with sticks ready for field hockey, girls in prom dresses with corsages, girls in ballet slippers and frazzled tutus, girls with new bikes.

In the front room, wearing dungarees and a denim jacket, was the young woman from the hospital — or half of her — for now she was as thin as her Robert had been. She sat on an old brown sofa, weighted down with a shotgun across her lap. "Hi," Basil Stein said. The girl didn't answer or look up.

The patrolmen came in and after shutting the windows, pulled the blinds and curtains. Immediately the house became very hot. Basil Stein sat on the sofa, tilting the thin girl toward him. "How about a snack, uh?" he said to Mirna.

She went out to the kitchen. A policeman sat at the table staring at the woman who was now handcuffed, both hands and feet, to the washing machine, and at the two men on the floor. Mirna looked in the refrigerator and cabinets and all she could find were a jar of peanut butter and a box of animal crackers. Basil Stein, Roy, and the patrolmen ate all of it and drank a gallon of water from a plastic pitcher with little cheese spread glasses.

Basil Stein brushed crumbs off his jacket and dabbed his mouth with a black silk handkerchief. He stood and nodded to Roy. Roy jumped up. "Good-bye," Basil Stein said. They shook hands.

Opening his mouth wide, Roy laughed and cried. Basil Stein turned and motioned to Mirna. She went to him and he put his arms around her. He kissed her and murmured, "It's a whole line of nature, there'll be peace in the valley." Then he and the patrolmen ducked out the back door and ran up the alley.

The girl turned on the TV, a big color set: there was a small yellow house with a low wall around it. The afternoon sun slanting down the street made the house, the runt trees, the sky itself, parched brown. "That's us," the girl said. She hooked back a curtain and up the street Mirna saw the TV men behind an old car, the camera on a fender. The men ran between some houses and, turning to the set Mirna saw hundreds of policemen milling on the back porches and in the yards across the street. Some sat on the hoods and trunks of patrol cars eating from lunch pails; many had taken off their shirts and were putting on vests of linked steel. Several pitched horseshoes in the alley, while others had spread army blankets and sat cleaning their machine guns. More motorcycle patrolmen and several patrol cars full of men came up the alley, and these joined the others without speaking, though the camera caught the sidelong glances, winks, and secret smiles the officers exchanged.

"Here," Roy said and handed Mirna a machine gun.

"I know nothing about these things," Mirna said.

"It's easy." He picked up another gun, crammed in a clip, wound the strap around his left arm, brought the stock to his shoulder, flicked off the safety, and with the snout of the gun hooked back the curtain. While he stared at Mirna with his depthless gray eyes, he pulled the trigger.

Instantly the air solidified. Continuous, profoundly dense noise locked thought. Mirna dropped her machine gun and covered her ears. She kept moving her feet up and down, even after she had backed against a wall, and there she stood, holding her breath, until Roy emptied the clip.

Through the numb ringing Mirna heard gunfire across the street, loud but strangely hollow.

The window panes shattered and the curtains and blinds twitched like skirts on the hips of mad dancers, and everything in the house was jerking, spurting into disintegration, chairs and little tables hopping and kicking over as pieces spewed out of splintered gouges. The sofa disgorged clots of stuffing. Pictures flew into pieces and hunks of plaster crashed to the floor. The TV set took a shot in the side and went red, gave a powerful moo, and exploded. In minutes the curtains and blinds were shredded, and in the brown light Mirna watched the living room and dining room become a long box of dust and rags.

"Whooee!" Through the dust Mirna saw the two black men stumbling through the kitchen and out the back door, carrying the washing machine with the woman riding on it.

The girl crawled through the debris, and Mirna got down on her hands and knees and followed her. They had just reached the bedroom door when a red-hot tin can came spinning through the window. Then another, then all at once half a dozen more, all skipping and leaping about, butting into what remained of the walls, and spewing tear gas.

In the bedroom closet the girl opened a trap door and crawled down the hole. Mirna followed.

In the crawl space there was the cool smell of earth and dry wood. The shooting was so remote, Mirna wondered if the police had decided to attack the house next door, having finished with this one.

But when the girl and Mirna reached a vent in the foundation, Mirna saw that the police were still across the street and still firing — and the day was becoming even browner as smoke buried the sky. The girl poked her shotgun out the vent, fired once, and the recoil kicked her skimming like a board back into the darkness. Immediately there was a steady thudding against the foundation and some bullets zipped through the vent and gouged up puffs of dust in the sandy earth.

Roy came down through the trap door. "Everything's on fire!" he shouted and crawled up beside Mirna. "What will happen?" he yelled.

The floor above was hot and through it they heard fire, a steady, increasingly loud rumble. "Dig!" Mirna yelled and clawed the sand. Roy dug beside her, scooping out sand between his legs like a dog. He shoved his face into the shallow hole, and cupped sand over his ears and neck.

Mirna climbed onto him, her back nearly touching the floorboards, and to her amazement in an instant all the air went straight up through the back of her head, neck, through her buttocks, and the length of her legs. It went out with a stunning suck that left her cold and expectant, her mouth open but airless, her eyes open and for a moment seeing nothing.

But then the vent was darkened by the shadow of an animal. Through the smoke, and looking out from such a tremendous distance within herself, it was as if she were looking up a misty forest path, Mirna barely saw the animal but knew it was a cat and knew it was of course none other than Pusser Boy. He stood in the air vent sniffing with that patient interest of cats, then he came slowly in and began licking Mirna's face. More, Mirna urged. More … And it was over, the cheetah trotting smoothly away, not glancing over its shoulder. Mirna leaned back and found as she expected, in the corner of the armrest where she would have left it, a slim volume with a slick black cover. She opened it and read the first lines, casually metered and rather obscure, rather private, concerning her life with heroes and villains.

LOVERS

PENNY LEAPED THE MORGANS' BACK YARD FENCE — she knew that would stop all of them but Danny. The rest of the children had to run up the fence and crowd through the gate. As she turned between the Morgan house and the Dunlap house she heard feet pounding behind her, and, turning the corner of the Dunlaps', she glanced over her shoulder and let out a trilling shriek when she saw Danny right behind her. She dodged around the corner, behind the shrubberies, and lost him for a moment. But when she ran from the shrubs, Danny lunged for her and they fell across the sidewalk, over the little wire fence, and into a deep bed of petunias.

The rest of the children came squealing around the corner, swarming through the shrubberies, and piled onto Penny and Danny, and they were all of them rolling around, giggling, touching Penny, their sweaty faces big-eyed, gleeful, when the screen door banged open and Mrs. Dunlap charged onto the porch, her bushy gray hair seeming to stand on end as if she were beholding wild animals in the act of seizing control of the neighborhood.

She came to the edge of the porch, faltered, her large mouth hanging open. Then she clenched a fist and struck her forehead. "Jesus God," she whispered.

One of the kids giggled. Penny and Danny scrambled to their feet.

Then it hit — but Penny was moving fast. She jerked one of the really little ones to his feet, and she didn't catch all Mrs. Dunlap was saying. But she caught the tone. Mrs. Dunlap was temporarily out of her mind — and she repeated that several times: "You've just plain driven me out of my mind, for God's sake."

They all climbed over the little wire fence and retreated to the street — expecting that at any moment Mrs. Dunlap would grab an arm, or the back of the neck, which was much worse; they all knew Mrs. Dunlap went for the back of the neck.

But when they reached the middle of the street they turned and saw

Mrs. Dunlap wasn't chasing them. Down in the flower bed on her hands and knees, Mrs. Dunlap was crying.

Penny giggled. But stopped. All the kids, even Danny, were very serious when they saw the woman down like that.

They stood there, and Penny felt the entire length of the block on both sides of the street hush with an awful intensification of the already somber quiet of dusk. She was glad her mother wasn't home.

"Why, oh why?" Mrs. Dunlap wept. "My lovely petunias. Why my *petunias?*"

"We're sorry, Mrs. Dunlap," Penny said.

"And *you*," Mrs. Dunlap said, slowly looking up from the trampled flowers, and Penny wished she had kept her mouth shut. "*You!* You little ..." She stopped herself. Penny wanted her to go on. She wanted very much to know what Mrs. Dunlap almost called her.

"Tell me," Mrs. Dunlap said, getting to her feet and coming across the yard to stand on her sidewalk, her fists on her wide hips. "Just tell me why you lead these little children to *do* such things as this. Why do you *play* with them? *Look* at you." The kids crowded around Penny. Danny turned and stared at Penny. She wanted to look down, but didn't. She just blinked her eyes once. "How old are you, young lady?"

"Thirteen."

"Thirteen years old. And you're all the time playing with these little tiny kids. Why, *look* at them. They're five and six years old and you're *playing* with them."

Danny's eleven, Penny wanted to say, but didn't.

"There must be something wrong with you. Why don't you play with children your own age?" She waited. "You're disgusting. You're *all* disgusting, running around after her like a pack of..." Mrs. Dunlap jerked her head to the side. For the rest of it, her railing at the kids for all their other crimes — beating down her grass and the grass of all the other yards in the neighborhood — Mrs. Dunlap avoided Penny's eyes. And Penny noticed that and she was puzzled, and it was funny — she laughed. When she did, the other kids laughed.

"This is *not* a laughing matter," Mrs. Dunlap said. She told them she was going into the house right this minute and call their parents.

"And when your mother gets home, young lady," she said, looking at Penny again, "I'll be right over and the three of us will have this *out once and for all.*"

But that didn't worry Penny — her mother wouldn't be back till tomorrow afternoon. But the threat worked on the little kids — most of them went straight home.

Penny and Danny, and Danny's little brother Mike, went up and sat on Penny's porch steps. They watched Mrs. Dunlap, in the flower bed again, pick up the limp corpses of her petunias and lay them in a pile. Mr. Dunlap came out and stood at the side of the porch. Penny could hear them talking low, though she couldn't hear the words. She watched Mr. Dunlap, bald and short, and she thought maybe he would look across the street at her, but he didn't. He only looked at her when he didn't think she would see him — and when she caught him, he would look away quickly. She always said, "Hello, Mr. Dunlap," when she happened to be out front as he backed his car out of his driveway, or when he was alone in his front yard, and he always answered her, but low, his head down, not looking at her, as if he didn't really mean it when he said hello.

Penny, Danny, and Mike rode Danny's and Mike's bikes for a while, Penny and Danny riding double, Penny behind Danny on the long banana seat, her large, smooth legs straddling Danny's narrow hips.

They sat on the porch again, talking, and Mike went home. After a while Danny followed Penny into her house.

James Morgan, from his window in the second floor of the house across the street, watched them go inside and then there was a heavy, dull blank.

He was unable to know what she was thinking when he couldn't see her. When she was playing in the street or in one of the yards, he could merely look at her closely — seldom blinking his eyes, hardly breathing — and inside himself he could hear her, hear every word she whispered to Danny, every thought that passed through her mind.

James knew what they did when she and Danny went inside her little house. First they went to the kitchen. Penny's mother worked at the A & P and she brought home big boxes of cookies. She and Penny ate gingersnaps and cream-fills all the time. So Penny and Danny went into the kitchen and ate some cookies, and then they came out to the front room and listened to the Beatles on Roy's stereo. Roy was Penny's mother's fiancé. Then sometimes they went into Penny's tiny bedroom, crowded with stuffed rabbits and giraffes, and Penny would take off her clothes, all but her bikini panties and bra, and she would lie on her bed, stretched out, and while Danny sat in the little rocking chair by the bed, Penny would tell him about men and women.

But James could only see them. He couldn't hear Penny, no matter how hard he stared at the house and the pink and white curtain, always closed, over the window in Penny's bedroom.

James waited, hoping Penny and Danny would come out again, but once they went into the house, they would stay for a long time, and when the front door eventually opened, Danny would come out alone.

But James could hear Danny and know what he was thinking no matter how far away he went. When Danny and Mike and some of the other boys went up to the park to play, James always knew where they were and exactly what they were doing — he could listen closely and hear what Danny was thinking as he played baseball or as he swam when they all went to the pool.

Danny came Tuesday afternoons to visit James. They played checkers and sometimes Fascination or Monopoly. James' favorite was Monopoly, but Danny didn't like it — it took too long. "There's going to be a new fourth grade teacher next year," Danny said. "My aunt knows her. She just got out of college. It's your move."

They were playing checkers and James played slowly, being careful with his moves.

"Miss Wilson is going to California. She's going to live with her mother," Danny said. "Can you imagine being that old and going someplace to live with your mother?"

James moved. Danny moved quickly and again waited for James.

"They had to make Miss Wilson quit. There's something wrong with her. It's your move. Probably being a teacher is what did it to her. Always fighting with me and Rodney Pearson and George Getz. Your move."

James moved. Danny quickly moved one of his kings, and as soon as he did James jumped that king and another, leaving Danny just one man on the board to James' five. "Geez," Danny said, shaking his head, his handsome face grimaced into a wrinkled imitation of his father's.

"Let's play another one," James said.

"Uh uh," Danny said, shaking his head, not looking at James. "I got to go."

"You just got here. It's just twenty after one and you got here at five minutes to one."

"I don't care. I got to go. I'm supposed to meet some guys."

"Who?"

Danny acted as if he hadn't heard. Then he glanced at James and said, "What?"

"Who are you going to meet?"

"Some guys. You don't know them. They don't live around here. I'm going to meet them up at the park. We're starting up a league." He looked out the window at the sun, bright on the maple tree below James' window.

James' mother tried to get Danny to stay a little longer, play another game of checkers and have some cake — the icing was cooling on a chocolate cake, it had probably set long enough, she would go down and cut them both a piece... But Danny couldn't stay. Sorry. He had to meet those guys, and he didn't look at James as he pushed the table back. And he pushed the table too far — it jolted James' bed, making a strange, hollow *koong*, and Danny looked away, embarrassed.

While James ate a piece of chocolate cake with ice cream, he looked out the window. In a few minutes Danny came down the sidewalk with Mike. They had their baseball gloves, and both wore new red baseball caps. They crossed the street to Penny's. Danny knocked and they talked when she came to the door, barefooted and wearing cutoff jeans and a tight sweater. Danny was asking Penny to go with him and Mike to play baseball, and James knew Penny was glad he asked her, for it meant that someday he would ask her to marry him and they would live in this block and have children who would ride their bikes up and down and play bounce ball until they were big enough to go to the park and play real baseball and ...

Penny went into the house and Danny and Mike waited on the porch, talking, Danny socking his fist into his glove. Then Penny came out. She was still barefooted, but she had changed to tight red shorts and a white halter. They headed up the street, and by the time they reached the corner five or six little kids were tagging along.

And James lay back and with his eyes half closed, staring out the window at the top limbs of the maple tree bobbing slightly in a breeze that seemed to touch only some, not all, of the leaves, he was with Penny, Danny, and Mike, and when they got to the park the other guys were already there.

The baseball diamond and the swimming pool, at opposite ends of the park, were separated by picnic tables and benches scattered under enough trees to make a forest when the kids needed one, and two stone toilets where last summer Penny had taken off all her clothes and let some of the kids look at her, and where with lipstick she had drawn a picture of a naked woman on the wall and under it written her name and the phone number of the police station.

The other guys knew Penny. They were in the same grade with her and they didn't like her — over a year ago they nicknamed her Pigpen Penny. But since today was the first day of the new league, they needed some extra players so they let Penny play, and they also let a couple of the little kids play in the outfield, even though they didn't have gloves.

Penny and Danny weren't on the same side, and while Danny sat waiting his turn at bat he tried not to watch Penny — this was baseball and he had to pay attention to what his team was doing. But he couldn't help but look at her now and then. Playing second base, she stood on the bag with one foot, the other leg bent and its bare foot pressed against the calf of the other leg, and she took off Danny's glove and tossed it into the air and caught it without losing her balance. The other guys were watching her too. Now she was giving little tugs to the tight legs of her shorts. Suddenly she became very interested in the game. She started chattering, hopping around second base, barking encouragement to her teammates. Then the kid at bat hit a line drive at her and she turned and ran. The ball hit her on one of the soft round cheeks of her butt. Everyone laughed. They laughed so hard they fell down and rolled around. When they stopped, her team's pitcher waved in one of the little kids from the outfield. The pitcher took Danny's glove from Penny and gave it to the little kid, and sent Penny out to right field.

But Penny got bored in right field and wandered off to the girls' toilet and they were able to forget about her for a while. Then as if from very far away they heard her, her voice high and cool.

"Oh Danny. Yoo hoo. Dannnnn-y."

He tried to ignore her, but everyone, even the little kids, got mad and started telling him to make her shut up.

"Shut up," he yelled.

But she kept it up. "Dannnnn-y. Yoo hoo."

Until his face was red and wrinkled, and he yelled so loudly he could have been heard clear to the swimming pool, "Shut up, dammit. Leave me alone. You're a big fat stupid pig. I hate you."

And suddenly she was as cold as the stone walls of the girls' toilet. She stood looking straight ahead at the walls, the names, faces, the dirty words, the pictures of wonderful, horrible men and gaping witches, and she put on her clothes.

When she came out of the toilet she didn't look at them, but headed the other direction, through the forest, where she felt the same strange coldness, as if winter lurked here in the woods, watching the children. She walked to the swimming pool and some of the little kids came over to talk to her. But they were just little kids.

James was waiting for her when she came down the sidewalk looking at the houses as she walked along. It was a strangely silent afternoon, the only sound the whisper of the water sprinklers. She sat on the porch of the little house where she lived, and once she glanced up at James' window. And as she looked into his eyes, though she couldn't see him, James stared back at her, unblinking, and knew that for the first time in her life Penny was lonely: she knew as completely as she ever would that she would be a woman all her life, and she was stunned.

They played baseball all summer and they even got uniforms — polo shirts with numbers which their mothers sewed on. Danny — number 3 — was the pitcher for one of the teams, and he pitched every game. At the height of the season they played four, five games a day, starting early in the morning and sometimes not stopping until suppertime — and then, likely as not, there was a game after supper.

And James and Penny were alone. She played bounce ball with the little kids in the block and rode double with them on their bikes, and sometimes

125

she babysat Mrs. Clark's twins. At night Danny and Mike occasionally played hide and seek with Penny and the little kids. One night when they were playing, some junior high boys came around and Penny stopped playing and went down to the corner and talked to them. When they left and Penny came running back, Mike was still playing hide and seek, but Danny had gone home.

A tall, gaunt boy with long black hair — James never learned his name — came to see Penny about every night for a week. He played hide and seek with her and the little kids. He laughed a lot and Penny laughed at everything he said. And then one morning he came to see Penny and they went into her house. James knew what they did was what Penny had done with Danny, except James knew Penny didn't take the tall, gaunt boy into her bedroom and she didn't take her clothes off and let him look at her.

One afternoon Danny was up at the park playing baseball and a kid on the other team started talking about Penny and the tall, gaunt boy. They had got in her bed with their clothes off. The baseball game stopped and they listened. When the kid had told everything — and some parts twice — they all stood in silence. How had he heard it? The tall, gaunt kid, who would be a sophomore in high school next year, had told a bunch of guys, and now anybody in high school who wanted to could go over to Penny's and do it to her.

The game resumed. Danny pitched, concentrating, leaning into every pitch, sweating, not thinking, his team ahead 8-4, the endless afternoon safe from time, a fine dust and the smell of fresh-cut grass floating on the air, the sun high in the perfectly blue sky...

He turned from the batter, dropped the ball, and walked off the mound.

"Hey."

"What's the matter?"

He shook his head.

Several of them trotted after him.

He walked straight through center field, hearing now very clearly the kids at the swimming pool, and it occurred to him that never before when he was playing ball had he heard the kids at the pool, and he looked up at the sky, clear blue, blank.

Danny walked down the sidewalk, tossed his glove onto the front porch as he passed his house, and James from his window watched him coming down the street in his red shirt with number 3 in front, his faded red cap, his arms tanned smooth like dark stone. He walked not fast, not slow, as if he were on his way to the grocery store, but James knew, and in front of Penny's, Danny turned up the sidewalk, swinging his arms, not looking up, and he went up the steps, crossed the porch, and he didn't knock but opened the door and went in, shutting it slowly behind him with a quiet, luminous click that James heard as he closed his eyes.

All the blinds were pulled and the house was dark. It had the smell of cigarettes and sour clothing. The front room was very small — smaller than Danny had ever noticed — and the ceiling seemed strangely low. The walls were brown, nearly black, and the chairs and lumpy sofa hunkered against the walls. As he passed through to the tiny hall joining the front room with the other three rooms of the house, he heard a drawer open, then close.

Wearing shorts and a sleeveless yellow blouse, Penny was coming out of her bedroom. Her mouth fell open, but she didn't speak. They stared at each other, the hall, the entire house, narrowing to the tight lines of their staring, and Danny moved first, going toward her like a ship slowly turning to sea. "What ... ?" she started, and he stopped her, his face in hers, and he smelled her, and smelled her mouth and saw deep into the slow swirl of her eyes, leaning forward until he was falling away, he was already into her and rising like gray smoke from the little boys' prison of innocence into weather that blew him toward life.

James watched the pink and white curtain of the bedroom. Once he believed it moved very slightly. But if it did, it didn't move again until it came down several months later when Penny's mother moved herself and Penny out with the help of a new fiancé with a pick-up truck, and for years James watched the house and that window, sometimes covered by curtains, sometimes by blinds, and once the window had nothing over it and James could see in the narrow room a table piled with cardboard boxes.

In time he lost interest in the neighborhood and what they were thinking: he knew them too well. James spent most of his time watching television, soap operas, baseball in the summer, and for a year or so he avidly watched the wrestling matches. Now when he looked out the window it was either to watch for the newspaper boy, late in the afternoon, even after dark in the winter, or it was to look out at the sky through the limbs of the maple tree.

MR. TANGIBLE

A HEAD POPS UP BEYOND THE DRIVEWAY HEDGE and from the dining room window Frankie watches the man sneak up on Ruth. Though he has never seen him before, Frankie knows this is Ruth's Mr. Tangible.

In the back yard Ruth moves through The Archer, her body gleaming with sweat as she draws the invisible bowstring farther, farther … leaning so far backward she is on the verge of tipping all the way into Elude Distractions. She releases the bowstring and smoothly rises up, her left arm rolling as she does, her wrist slowly rotating her hand in a beckoning motion, one by one her fingers curling closed with a Come hither to the head peering over the hedge, though she hasn't once looked his way.

She takes a deep breath and steps into the shade of the mulberry tree in the center of the yard and lies down on a plastic chaise lounge, her arms hanging down, legs apart, feet pointing slightly outward.

Frankie knows that Ruth is aware Mr. Tangible is there, for when she finishes working out she usually comes straight in and takes a shower. So now Ruth is giving him his chance. Mr. Tangible wipes his broad, red forehead with a handkerchief, obviously trying to decide if he wants his chance. Go ahead Frankie thinks hard, and with a nod sends it out the window ahead, repeating it so rapidly the separate darts of thought concentrate into a continuous, intense jet aimed straight across the driveway and trained on Mr. Tangible's forehead.

Charles Wilson prepares to raise hell. Mavis Conklin, the next-door neighbor who phoned yesterday to complain, was right about the carrying on, as she called it, over here on Yucca Way — not only nakedness, but naked shows in the back yard in broad daylight.

Though this morning at breakfast Charles didn't give his wife Ida all Mavis Conklin's details. He just said he intended to evict the tenant on Yucca Way and added, "Do you want to come with me?"

"Huh," Ida said. She was eating oatmeal. When Charles asked her again she looked at him and said, "Why should I want to do that? I've got better fish to fry than going over to Yucca Way. Huh."

Charles had known better than to rent to the woman, Ruth Rink. But she reminded him of someone, though he doesn't know who — and he let himself feel sorry for her, though he isn't sure why. He's not one to feel sorry. At church he gives to foreign missions, and as for people here in the U.S. it's Charles's belief that anyone can do all right if he just straightens out his life. Anyone who doesn't straighten out his life must be satisfied with some part of it. Charles has always believed that people are not only satisfied, down deep, with what they get but they moreover love it, good or bad.

Obviously she wasn't interested in straightening out her life, this Ruth Rink. Or that's what she claimed as her name. She looked foreign to Charles, Middle Eastern, or a little of this and a little of that. She could only pay part of a month's rent — she was having a run of bad luck, she said. And no, she didn't have a husband, she lived alone.

She was thin and sunken in, and her skin was fading, pale yellow. Her arms were thin and so bloodless they were gray, almost blue, earthen. While they talked she did something which Charles didn't understand at first, opening her mouth slightly and expelling little puffs of air. He thought she was coughing weakly, but then he realized she was trying to laugh at her luck. Her eyes had the gray look which people get when they are starving.

Charles unloaded her old station wagon and the lopsided whitewashed trailer she had pulled nonstop, she said, all the way from Flagstaff. Then he went to the Alpha Beta and stocked her up with groceries.

As he carried in the grocery bags and even put things in the refrigerator — his own, which came with the house — the woman stood watching him as if she had never seen anything like this, her mouth shut tight, now, maybe afraid that if she said the wrong thing he would take it all back. Finally she asked how he expected her to pay for all this.

Charles said she should just consider it a turn in her luck. "I have a feeling," he said, "that things are starting to look up for you." He put his hand on her shoulder. It was intended to show kindness to someone in need of a friend. But the instant he touched her he knew it was the wrong thing to do, a stupid thing to do. He got out of there as fast as he could.

Early the next morning he was out front. He would just drop in to see how she was doing. Sure. He pulled into the driveway but stopped halfway

130

in and asked himself just what the hell he was doing. He backed out and drove on to the lumber yard.

So now the neighbors are complaining and it's time for Charles to go ahead and raise hell and evict her. He'll start with "Just who the hell do you think you are?"

But instead of yelling at the naked woman, Charles comes around the hedge and crosses the driveway into the sunny yard. He goes right up to where she lies on the chaise lounge and he looks down at her shining body, and she smiles up at him, not at all surprised at his sudden appearance.

The three of them sit on the patio shaded by the web of the biggest spider Charles has ever seen. When he offers to kill it with a board, Frankie says, "Go ahead," at the same time Ruth says, "No way! Mr. Spider is my buddy."

"Huh," is Charles's reply, and he can hear Ida whisper in his ear, You just better watch your step, Buster Brown.

"When we lived in Phoenix," Ruth says, "we had a spider as big as a dog."

Both watch their Mr. Tangible nod as if he expected this, as if he has conversations like this all the time. Frankie turns to Ruth and says, "Why don't I remember that? I don't remember that at all. You've just told a goddamned lie."

"Just because you can't remember it doesn't mean it's a lie, Sweetheart," Ruth says. "You can't remember it because you weren't there. There are a lot of things you can't remember because you weren't there."

Frankie's pretty little face burns with anger at being embarrassed in front of company. Or that's how Charles sees it. Skinny and sickly pale, with dirty blond hair that is long and greasy-green and hangs straight down, Frankie is certainly not a child but appears to be stuck at that age when boys are as pretty as girls. Charles isn't sure what Frankie is, boy or girl, but because Frankie is wearing a little brown cotton dress Charles assumes he is looking at a girl.

Ruth and Frankie argue about other places which Frankie doesn't remember. It's obvious to Charles that Frankie tries to watch out for her mother. But of course the job is too much for her, poor kid. How can a child be expected to make her mother act responsibly and show respectability? It was Frankie who earlier brought a white silk robe out to the patio for Ruth, and nagged her until she put it on.

When Charles had walked across the driveway into the yard, Ruth lay there looking up at him and didn't cover her nakedness. Charles talked. He can't remember what he said, though when he finished he started over and said everything again. She got up from the chaise lounge and stood in front of him, close. Charles's heart blundered around inside him, swollen up and trying to get out. Was she going to do something right out there in the yard? She turned and he followed her, watching her hips and small waist, to the house.

When Charles had looked up he saw someone in the kitchen, a narrow man barely visible inside the dark house. Well, it didn't take her long to grab hold of a man, Charles thought. Now she'll be able to pay her damned rent — and Charles would make her pay for the damned groceries, too.

Something was vaguely familiar about the face looking out of the dark house, and as Charles tried to place exactly what it was his heart missed some beats and slowly rolled over the way your heart does when someone walks across your grave, as they say happens, as Ida says happens. Then Charles realized the person standing inside wasn't a man at all but a skinny little girl in a brown dress. When Ruth introduced them, she said Frankie had arrived last night, "In the middle of the night," she said, her arm around Frankie's waist. "Nothing like a big surprise for Mama, isn't that right, Sweetheart?"

Ruth sends Frankie into the house for a little jug of brandy. When she brings it out, Ruth sends her back in to get them something to eat. Frankie goes into the house, glaring over her shoulder at them.

"Well," Ruth says. "Mr. Tangible. Tell me all about yourself."

Charles laughs solidly, as if he is used to being talked to like that, and replies, "Tangible assets? Is that what you mean?"

Ruth laughs in exactly the same way, which Charles takes as not only her answer but her showing she is pleased with how quickly he picks up on things, and pleased with him, too.

"Okay, then. All about Mr. Tangible. Mr. Tangible!" He laughs and she laughs with him, and when he reaches out and touches his brass cup of brandy she reaches out and touches hers at exactly the same time. "Well, Ruth, all right. But I'm not much of a talker."

"There's no hurry," she says. "We have all the time in the world."

Charles has the feeling she doesn't mean that — that she wants him right away, that she doesn't want to wait, though if he left and didn't return for a week, that would be all right with Ruth, that anything, actually, is all right with her. But she would prefer Mr. Tangible to come a little faster. Maybe this morning when she woke up she knew that today was the day for him, for Mr. Tangible, that he would come around, just as he did.

All this is some kind of game, that's clear to Charles. But it's difficult for him to hold back from easing all the way into it with her. It's all so familiar, as if they're old acquaintances. Though Charles suspects he shouldn't, he lets himself slide into believing he knows at the back of his mind what he's doing. It certainly helps that today Ruth looks so much better than on the day Charles rented the house to her. She looks no less foreign now than she did then, but now she is beautiful, her face small- featured, intricate — so intricate that Charles feels that even as he stares at it he can't get, can't absorb, as much of it as he wants, that merely looking at her face, seeing it, isn't enough. Before, she was starving, near death as they say, only a week ago she was dead on her feet as they say, as starving people can die while you watch them standing before you. But now she is beautiful, confident, she can see through her problems and the people who cause them.

They drink thick yellow brandy and use chopsticks to spear balls of tofu from brown soup. Charles watches how Ruth does it, and stays in rhythm with her, grinning, his mouth full of tofu, and he picks up his bowl when she picks up hers to drink soup.

"I guess this is how they do it in your country," Charles says.

"My country?" Ruth laughs. "Sure. How do they do it in your country?"

When they finish, Charles closely watches Frankie stack the bowls and gather the chopsticks. Too closely, staring, Charles watches Frankie carry the things into the house and bring out another little jug of brandy.

"I'm not used to drinking in the middle of the day, Mr. Tangible says. He smiles clearly at Frankie, sure that it's clear to both of them, and he is ashamed of himself at the same time he doesn't care.

Ruth says, "I want to show you something," and rises slowly from the table and Charles rises in the same way, leaning forward slightly, while the two of them look across at each other, and when Ruth moves her hands down her hips, smoothing the white silk robe along her hips, Charles's hands on their own reach toward her. She takes one of Mr. Tangible's big square hands and leads him into the house. "Here," she seats him on a mattress, "Now, like this . . ." and leans him back on silk cushions.

Frankie goes into the bedroom, doesn't close the door all the way. Through a mirror which makes them seem quite far away he watches Ruth hand Mr. Tangible the jeweled goblet carved from a skull. He turns it upside down for a look at the bottom — as if to see if it says where it was made. He holds it in front of his face — that's rich, they're eye to eye. Frankie waits for him to say something to it, but all he can manage is "Huh." Instead of lifting it as if he is drinking from it, or asking to have it filled up he'll drink from it, or asking where it came from and who it was, Mr. Tangible says, "What's it for?"

"It's a goblet," Ruth says. "For drinking."

"Huh. That's what I thought." He sees the inscription on the skull, squints, trying for better light he turns it this way and that. Frankie hears him thinking *What does this mean?* But he doesn't look long enough or think hard enough to make out what it means. When Ruth turns on the music Mr. Tangible sets the skull aside, it's just another thing.

The music comes softly from a speaker in the attic. Mr. Tangible lifts his head, his mouth hanging open, his head cocked to the side straining to hear. As the music becomes slightly louder his mouth shapes his gape of appreciation — he almost recognizes this, or at least he believes he does. Then there is a great pulsation under the mattress he is lying on, from under the house, like a ground swell or earthquake — but it is sound, many speakers, or one huge speaker in the crawlspace under the house. Slowly, ponderously it pulsates like a great heart and music comes from all around him, bright, tinkling bells and those string instruments from India ... what are they? — sitars, yes, a lot of them all going at once, fast music, excited to the point of frenzy. "My God," Mr. Tangible says. "If it starts like this what will it . . .?"

The music lightens like rain abruptly abating and Frankie enters, a

134

dancing girl, which surprises and of course delights Mr. Tangible — and assures him that he knows what they're up to, for he would have bet a hundred dollars Frankie would come out like this, dressed like a dancing girl, and — see? — he would have won his bet.

"Oh Daddy, Daddy," she sobs softly, she wants her daddy, she wants to know where he is and who he is. "Are you my daddy?" she whispers. "Sure," Mr. Tangible whispers. It's not a whole lie because of course she already knows that he isn't her daddy. If he was her daddy . . .

Mr. Tangible glances at Ruth lying on the other side of him, spread out and snoring, her white silk robe fallen open and her beautiful body, even in sleep, poised in something like one of the movements in her workout.

Turning back to Frankie he whispers, "I'm not your official father but I'll be just like a father to you." She stops crying, "You will?" "Sure. I'm going to take care of you and your mama. You don't need to worry about anything." He leans his face closer to her little face. God, she's beautiful. With Mr. Tangible watching so closely, Frankie cries some more, silently. Mr. Tangible watches tears fill her eyes and tears flow into her hair. Mr. Tangible brushes away the tears and before he knows it Frankie has slipped into his arms and he is kissing her. They kiss silently, without moving, the two of them looking intently into each other's eyes.

When it is time to go, Mr. Tangible lets Ruth undo his buckle and slowly tug his belt from around his waist. He grins — a souvenir, he figures, she wants a memento. He lets her do it. His pants won't fall down, he doesn't really need a belt, he just wears one because men wear belts. Then Ruth steps closer to him and he slides his arms around her in that white silk robe and they kiss. After they have kissed and are holding each other, Frankie comes up behind Ruth, leans up, Mr. Tangible and Frankie kiss for just as long as Ruth and he kissed. Then Frankie backs away, lips parted, frail — Frankie is sick, it occurs to Mr. Tangible, the poor kid has some kind of disease. Mr. Tangible hopes he didn't catch it when he kissed her. The poor kid is so frail and sick she can hardly make it to the bedroom door and the darkness beyond it.

He is over there again of course the next day. He intended to wait at least a week — Mavis Conklin next-door never misses anything that goes on and Charles certainly doesn't want rumors flying around town about him and the poor woman who rents from him on Yucca Way and her pitiful little girl.

Charles takes reasonable precautions. He brings a stepladder in his pickup and makes a lot of noise unloading it and his tool box. When Ruth comes to the back door Charles talks loudly about fixing those loose floorboards.

Hammering away with one hand and making a hell of a racket on Mavis Conklin's side of the house, Mr. Tangible puts his other arm around Ruth and kisses her, and when she goes to the kitchen Frankie comes up for a turn and Mr. Tangible leans down and bends the little wisp of a thing up against him as he holds her and kisses her little face, forcing his big tongue into her little mouth, which fills it up completely, which makes him so dizzy he swings wild with the hammer and breaks out a window. "God damn!" he exclaims. Frankie jumps back. Ruth comes out of the kitchen. Mr. Tangible sees Mavis Conklin peering at him out a window in her house. She is big but has tiny eyes like a bird, she is a thick fat bird that has halfway become a different species, one too big to fly, that armors itself with slabs of meat.

"That's all right," Mr. Tangible says, "I'll fix it. Don't worry."

Later he reclines on the silk cushions and Ruth feeds him crunchy little splintery things. "Come on," he urges her, he wants a whole handful, but she only drops one at a time into his mouth and lets him barely wet his lips with the jeweled goblet carved from a skull, full of thick yellow brandy. The music begins and Frankie the little harem girl comes out to dance, slowly and reluctantly, her dirty little head bowed in shame.

Mr. Tangible leans back and closes his eyes. "Oh God, how I love this," he says. He asks Ruth if he has died and gone to heaven. "Is that possible?" he says and answers himself, "Anything is possible."

Frankie catches Mr. Tangible's hair in a brass basin as Ruth cuts it. Mr. Tangible says, "Not too short," and laughs good- naturedly, for of course when Ruth is finished and holds a blue mirror before him he's as bald as a baby. His eyes shift to Ruth's and he says, "Huh? What's that?"

Ruth murmurs, "You know there's no way I can repay you."

Waving her off, Mr. Tangible says, "Are you kidding? It's yours, don't you see? Isn't there some way I can make that clear to you?"

136

Ruth reaches out with the scissors, Mr. Tangible holds perfectly still, and she snips off the lobe of his left ear.

He gasps, jerks back. Frankie puts her cold little mouth over Mr. Tangible's ear. "God, that feels good," Mr. Tangible says, his voice sounding strange to him with his ear inside Frankie's mouth. Mr. Tangible laughs and says softly, "I'd like to just go everywhere with Frankie hanging from my ear. Do you think you can arrange that?" he asks Ruth.

Ruth smiles in a new way, a rather crooked, rather ironic smile that, coming when it does, he doesn't understand, though it seems that Ruth's smile suggests a degree of dissatisfaction with Mr. Tangible, as if there could be more, a lot more, if he cared, if only Mr. Tangible really cared. I'll show her, he tells himself when he kisses them goodnight. It's early evening, he stayed longer than he intended and there will be hell to pay when he gets home- — kissing first Ruth, then holding her while Frankie stands close behind her, almost touching her but not quite, and opening her mouth for a good reaming with Mr. Tangible's big tongue.

He got his hair caught and cut his ear in the circle saw at the lumber yard, then he had to go to the doctor's, that's why he's so late. Ida believes him, doesn't seem awfully surprised, as if all along she expected that someday he would have trouble with the circle saw.

Later at Wednesday evening services when Charles feels something cold on his neck he shivers and gasps and almost laughs out loud when the thought rushes into his mind that Frankie has sneaked into the church, crawled under the pews all the way up to the front row where Mr. Tangible is sitting beside Ida, and has risen up behind him and is trailing her cold, sharp little tongue down his neck. But what he feels on his neck isn't Frankie's tongue but blood running down inside the collar of his shirt. He cups his hand over his ear, as if to better hear the minister's every word.

The next day he goes back early in the morning with a pane of glass to put in the broken window. "As promised!" he says when Ruth comes to the back door.

She wears a dark green silk robe. She doesn't smile or even say hello. "Well, you don't seem awful happy to see Mr. Tangible," he says. It occurs to him she has someone in the bedroom. He almost blurts out an accusation, but stops himself. If there is someone in there he would just as soon not know. "Don't you think," he says when she finally unhooks the screen door and lets him in, "that I've earned a little more appreciation from you?"

She goes into the bedroom and shuts the door.

Mr. Tangible puts in the new window pane, his every move watched by Mavis Conklin, and when he is finished he picks up his hammer and slowly pushes it through the glass. Did Mavis Conklin see that? Yep. There she is, looking at him, her mouth open with amazement.

Mr. Tangible takes off the baseball cap which he plans to wear until his hair grows out. He shakes his head, and says out loud, "Well, I guess I'm just about the clumsiest person in the world."

He drops the hammer to the floor, crosses the room, and opens the bedroom door. Ruth and Frankie are side by side in bed, their heads on the same pillow, the covers pulled up to their necks. Mr. Tangible knows that under the covers they're naked as jaybirds — Ruth and Frankie, the loves of his life.

Later that day, before sundown but long after the boys at the lumber yard have closed for the day, wondering when they'll see Charles again, Mr. Tangible walks with great dignity down the driveway of his rental property on Yucca Way, his right hand lifted in front of him, drawing attention to itself, the fingers fidgeting industriously, eager to get to work at something, anything, while the other hand tucks itself against his side to conceal the fact that three fingers, including the thumb, are gone.

Ida agrees he should stay home a few days if he has gotten so clumsy he can't do a day's work without injuring himself.

So he lies around the house, very quiet, a lot quieter and more contented than Ida would have expected — he's so quiet she hardly knows he's there. Then on the second day of his convalescence when Ida goes into the parlor to ask him what he wants for supper, she discovers he's gone.

Of course he's gone. He's in the back yard of the house on Yucca Way with Ruth learning Secret Wind. Though he has never in his life gone outdoors without clothes on, here he is in broad daylight and not only is he naked, he is about to embarrass himself the way he did in high school every time he took a shower after gym class. He tries to ignore it, but that is no more successful than when he was a boy.

He gets the hang of Secret Wind, but when Ruth leads him into Elude

Distractions he wants to stop because of his embarrassing condition, but she says Go ahead, and when he is bent all the way back and hears Ruth say, far away, that he is locked in his flight pattern, and he feels that despite all he is indeed eluding distraction, Mr. Tangible sees, upside-down, coming toward him a small bald-headed man wearing a white bedsheet, a little Hindu holy man.

The little holy man is Frankie!

Frankie withdraws a hand from the sheet and Charles sees too late that she is carrying the butcher knife. Charles does his best, in the last few seconds, to think of something else, as he did when he was a high school boy to make his embarrassment go away. But, as always, that only encourages his embarrassment, causing it to become even bigger and waggle around as if eagerly waving and calling to Frankie and the knife, "Here I am! Here I am!"

By the time he recovered and could get out of bed his left arm just above the elbow was gone, too, sewed up with Ruth's black thread in a way that made it appear that his arm ended in lace, and on the place where his manhood had stood there was now a pad of lacy loops and spirals. Though he made a lot of noise, not words, not crying, to his surprise his mending passed quite quickly. Sleeping helped, the first few days after he knew for sure it was gone, really gone. In dreams he worked behind the counter at the lumber yard, and drove his pickup, and even danced with a girl at the high school prom and felt an embarrassment coming on, and he always awoke serene. Ruth lay beside him, snoring lightly, and on the other side of him, when he turned his head, Frankie's bright eyes stared through the dark.

"It's been a good life," he said out loud. What a hick he sounded like. He realized what a hick he was. "Why don't you take that next?" he said. Ruth turned over in her sleep and stopped snoring, and Frankie didn't answer, though Charles knew they heard him.

A few days later Ruth returned from the bank with the news that Ida had closed the checking account. All three of them laughed. "You know what's next, don't you?" Mr. Tangible said.

"Right," Ruth said. "Ida herself!"

"No," Mr. Tangible said, and paused, wondering what Ruth meant by that. "No, Ruth. What comes next is the lawyer."

He was right. At eight o'clock sharp the next morning Lowell Tozier, attorney at law, came knocking and handed Ruth the papers which informed Mr. Tangible that Ida was suing him for divorce. Charles took this calmly, of course, for he was expecting it and also because he had become a master of calmness. Ruth, however, was upset.

"Talk about your heartless bitches!" Ruth yelled. She stormed up and down from one end of the house to the other, kicking things and giving forearm blows to the walls that made the house shudder. Mr. Fang the cat, new that week to the household, came flying into Charles's room, leaped up on the bed, its ears down and its eyes huge with alarm, then it leaped out the window, startling Mavis Conklin so much she fell back from her window, and in a lull in the racket Ruth was making, Mr. Tangible heard Mavis knock over the table where she set her coffee cup, ashtray, and phone.

Ruth rushed into the bedroom. "Damn her! I'm going over there. I'll show her!"

"Calm down, honey," Mr. Tangible said. "What's got you so riled up? Don't pay any attention to Ida. This is working out just as we planned. What more do you want?"

"It's her effrontery," Ruth said, "that's what galls me."

"After all, hon, she is my wife. Or at least she used to be."

"We're going to fight this all the way, goddamnit. I'll get a lawyer and we'll fight her every inch of the way if she thinks she's going to get everything you own."

"She probably just wants her fair share."

"What's fair about it? You know very well what she thinks her fair share is — everything you've got. Everything!"

"True enough, hon. You know Ida like a book. But I wouldn't feel right giving her nothing at all."

"Why not? That's exactly what Frankie and I had when we came here. Let her have a taste of what that's like."

"But it's not fair."

"Frankie!" Ruth screamed.

"Now, hon ..." Charles said, tugging the sheet up to his chin with his arm.

"Frankie!" and Charles heard Mavis Conklin's phone dial spin as she

140

started calling everyone as she did each time Ruth and Frankie set to work on Mr. Tangible, and he heard Frankie banging around in the kitchen looking in drawers and cupboards. She and Ruth had been up late last night and evidently she was hungover, poor kid, and having a heck of a time finding the butcher knife.

Ruth and Frankie got no settlement, for as soon as Charles appeared at the preliminary divorce hearing it was plain to Lowell Tozier and Ida that a divorce would be a big mistake. Ida could simply wait a while, by the looks of things only a week, two at most, and she would inherit everything.

That day at the hearing, which was the last time Ida saw him — or what was left of him — he was in a wheelchair, held in place with a belt around his narrow chest, with red silk pillows on both sides of him and one under him where he ended at the waist — actually he ended above the waist. All that was left was the narrow box where the essential parts cling to each other, and sitting on the box his poor shiny head and what was left of his face.

Ida didn't recognize him, she later told Lowell Tozier, and even wondered if in fact the person in the wheelchair had been Charles. Once, while the lawyers argued, Ida thought he looked at her across the big oblong table, but there was nothing in his eyes. Maybe he was blind. Or if he could see her he couldn't recognize her.

Ida had gone over to Mavis Conklin's more than once to look into that house. Ida's only consolation was that, though she was losing Charles to that crazy woman, she would have lost him anyway to this horrible disease that was taking him apart — disassembling him, as someone in town said — one piece at a time. Ida was losing him, but that woman wasn't getting him — or at least she wasn't getting much, it could be carried practically in one hand.

The night Ruth and Frankie loaded up the station wagon and lopsided old trailer they put Mr. Tangible on the kitchen table and had Mr. Fang tend to him. One last time they played the music as loud as it would play. Far away beyond the music Charles heard Mavis Conklin screaming, "Turn down that barbarian music." Crouching on the table, Mr. Fang dourly licked away a tear that rolled down Mr. Tangible's cheek.

When Ruth and Frankie came in, after everything they could take was loaded up, Ruth sat down at the table facing Mr. Tangible. She shoved Mr. Fang off the table and pulled Charles in front of her.

"Mr. Tangible," she said, smiling sadly. "Poor old Mr. Tangible. Well, honey, here we are again and your mama's hongry all over again just like she never ate nothin in her whole life. Now what do you think of that, huh? Huh? Frankie, show your daddy. See that, honey? That teensy weensie little gouger is the thang we use when we do brain surgery. You know? We go in there just like we're driving down the pike. Why, there's even a little head-light at the point-end of it so we can see and won't make any wrong turns."

Mr. Tangible shifted his eyes up at Frankie and his lip quivered, which Ruth and Frankie noticed and commented on, saying wasn't that sweet, Mr. Tangible's saying goodbye. "Well, goodbye to you, Sweet Pie," Ruth said and touched a finger to Mr. Tangible's cheek, careful not to topple him over.

"What'll it be?" Ruth asked Frankie. "Shall we listen to some nice sitar songs from Varanasi? Or how about 'Death and Transfiguration'? Or, hey, I've got it — 'Sergeant Pepper'!" She bent down and asked Mr. Tangible, "What do you think of that, honey? The good old Beatles! Isn't that just right — 'Sergeant Pepper'?"

Charles allowed it was just right and they commenced. As they excavated, probing deeper and deeper, Charles cried as the music spread over him like melted plastic, gold and green, and as he heard again the songs he loved so much when he was young he recalled how he felt when he had all of himself, he was seventeen years old again, strong and full of life, ready for anything, smoking his first cigarette, the entire world spreading out before him with at least sixty years of time, or so he had assumed, to do everything he might want.

He was still there when they finished. His eyes watched them stir fry his brain in a wok and eat it with chopsticks. Then they put a fire under the stew pot and boiled water. After his bath they wiped away the scraps of face remaining. Soon before them they had the big skull, Mr. Tangible, rock-hard and grinning at them.

Mavis Conklin dozed despite the awful music and when she woke at dawn the car and old trailer were gone. It was her bet that they had cleaned everything out. She went out straight over there. "Charles?" she called. "Yoo hoo. Charles?" When she tiptoed through the doorway — they had taken the door and even the hinges — she found nothing but debris in the kitchen and the other rooms. But she felt that poor Charles was still

142

here, somewhere. She looked up in the attic, even went outside and with a flashlight peered into the crawlspace under the house.

Back in the house she sat down on the kitchen floor and sifted through the debris and tiny scraps of paper, looking for a message.

PATSY O'DAY IN THE WORLD

THE WINDOWS FLOATED IN THE WATER OF DAWN and like a murky tide gray crossed the ceiling. Soft arms of gray slowly reached down into the room, gray bellies bulged from the ceiling until the room, a dark pool in which Patsy floated on her back, was filled with the same cold gray as the ceiling, the windows, the sky.

She got up and went to the window. Far below, the street was a black and gray canal. As always, there were people on the wide sidewalks. She opened a window and leaned out, as though she would call down and tell them it was all right for them to start now, she was awake, she was ready. But she didn't call down to them — it was cold and she closed the window and watched them, four men. Two stood in a dark doorway, another with folded arms leaned on a parking meter, the fourth sat on the curb. She leaned her forehead against the cold glass trying to see if perhaps one of them was Peter Gone. Yesterday he told her he would come back last night, but he hadn't. When they left she always wondered if she would see them again. But Peter Gone would come back. She was sure he would. She knew him — *knew* him. And she knew other people in the same deep way, a mysterious certainty that she never tried to explain to herself or anyone else. But she knew, and with this special knowledge she could love Peter Gone, with his soft, lonely eyes, and she would help him.

She went back to the mattress and lay down, her hands folded under her head, and she felt herself slipping out of the gray when she heard footsteps in the hall. Then the door opened. Mr. Moluska stuck his head in, looked around the big empty room, then stepped quickly in and shut and locked the door behind him. He was wearing the same old suit he always wore, gray and slick, and his wide-brimmed black felt hat which made his pale, long face even more weird. Coming toward the mattress, not looking at her yet but around the room at the posters and pictures covering the walls, he took off his coat, shirt, trousers, tisking as he frowned at the blue and orange dayglo "Up Nixon With The ABM." The last thing he took off

144

was his big black hat, and as he did he looked at Patsy and smiled, his old blue lips drawing back from his shiny teeth. Then he took out his teeth, put them in his hat, and set it beside the mattress. His old gray body jiggled rubbery as he knelt down on the mattress beside her.

He put his teeth back in his mouth and put on his hat. He sat crossed-legged, reached out and patted her. "I'm still like a young man, eh?"

"You sure are, Mr. Moluska."

"You know how I do it?"

"How?"

"I'm sixty years old and I never done nothing I didn't really want to do. You know what I'm saying?"

She nodded.

"That's the answer, chickie. You see this?" He held himself up for her to see, as if she hadn't already seen quite enough for one morning. "My friend is sixty years old like me. But it don't act it, right? It thinks it's thirty, forty years old. Maybe younger even." He nodded, looking down at himself fondly.

He glanced around the room at the posters and loudly glaring faces — saintly Ches, awed Vietnamese children naked amid smoking rubble, Malcom X staring rigidly at Mr. Moluska and Patsy. "Now this kind of thing ..." Mr. Moluska shook his head. "This makes my friend sad. You know? You've been here what is it two weeks? and already look at you." He shook his head. "And the one before you the same way. It's no good. Marry and be a wife. Stop all the groping. And that on your stomach. Cute. But it's stupid. Believe me you'll regret it," and he leaned forward to take another look at the dime-sized yellow butterfly tattooed near her navel.

"But after you there'll be another one and I'll see it all over again. What's your name I forgot."

"Patsy O'Day."

He nodded. "I'll forget again. About the time I learn your name they send another one." He turned to the posters again. "I told the last one not to put up these things." He looked at Patsy. "But she done it anyway. Why? So I tell her all right put them up but put them up with little pins, you know, those little pins that have the plastic ends on them, make little tiny holes. But no. She puts them up with the Scotch tape and she nails them up with nails this long. You know what it does to the walls?"

"When are you going to do something about the window panes, Mr. Moluska?" Patsy said softly.

"The window panes look at them you break them out for me to put more in, is that it?" He got up and strode across the room. Some of the small panes were broken out completely and replaced by squares of cardboard. Others were patched with black tape. "Two or three girls back, I put in all new panes and the next day I come up to see how they are and there's three, four panes broke out already and the girl says they had a big rally and the futz broke out the windows with their billy clubs."

"Fuzz."

"Eh?"

"Fuzz, Mr. Moluska."

"Fuzz to you too, chickie. You got a sweet box and a big heart too, you share, but no complaints about the window panes or I tell Mr. Russell it's quits and I'll move out your headquarters to the sidewalk. And your fuzz'll help me too, believe me."

Patsy sat in the middle of the mattress and watched as Mr. Moluska put on his clothes.

"What you say to that?" he said.

She smiled. "All right, Mr. Moluska."

He looked away, then quickly back at her as if he thought she would laugh at him when he turned away.

"Well I'll go now," he said.

"All right."

"You're a good chickie."

"Yes. You said."

He nodded. "Yes. Well, bye-bye."

"Bye-bye."

He unlocked the door, stuck his head out and looked up and down, then stepped out into the hall. His head popped back in. "Aren't you going to lock this door?"

She shook her head.

"You should lock your door. It's a city law. It fights crime. So lock it."

"I'm expecting friends. If I lock it, I'll just have to unlock it again."

146

"'Expecting friends. Believe me, chickie, you'll not see sixty. Not you.'" He waited for her to speak. She didn't. So he shrugged and shut the door.

The three young men had just sneaked back in from Canada and they told Patsy they were bounders — they demonstrated by locking arms and bounding across the floor with giant lunging hops, all six feet landing at the same time, shaking the room, the floor cracking and making splitting sounds. Patsy laughed and expected the floor to fall through. When they fell and rolled laughing on the floor, they heard the Cubans yelling in the apartment below. Patsy was pouring cups of broth for them as they sat on pillows on the floor telling her about the headquarters in Canada, and Senor Yero burst in shouting Spanish and shaking two big hunks of plaster in Patsy's face. He was a bony little man and his rage was pitiful — Patsy wanted to cry and put her arms around him. His whole body trembled as he shouted at her and shook the crumbling plaster at her and then at the three boys sitting on the floor, and he spluttered out a word or two of English. Tears ran down his cheeks and Patsy put her arms around him. He pushed her away, but he had calmed somewhat and Patsy apologized and made promises. "No hable Espanol," one of the fellows said and waved good-bye to him.

Then people started calling and Patsy was on the phone for a solid hour while the three bounders slept on the floor. Megan came around to leave a note for Bill if he showed up on his way to the new resistance office. The man upstairs started up his big electric sewing machine and a snow of fine powder started falling from the ceiling. The sewing machine woke the three bounders — they thought it was an airplane. Patsy phoned out some telegrams, charging them to one of the numbers Russell had listed in the big book Patsy used.

Tracy, Ralph, Max, and Louis came for a meeting, but the rest of their committee didn't come. Thanking Patsy for messing things up again — for she had set up the meeting — they left. They hadn't been gone ten minutes before George, Bob, and Woody, the rest of the committee, came in and they got mad at Patsy, too. They were yelling at her, they were going to tear up the place, and the three boys who were back from Canada woke, thought there was going to be a fight, and started slipping for the door, the last of them apologizing to Patsy for not staying around, explaining hastily that right now they couldn't afford a confrontation that might involve the fuzz because they had word the FBI was just two hops behind them. When George, Bob, and Woody heard that, they stopped yelling at Patsy and started talking to the three bounders, found they had mutual friends, and George, Bob, and Woody knew how they could help the three fellows make it to San Francisco, if they wanted to go to San Francisco — and sure enough they did want to go to San Francisco. Patsy made more broth and they all sat down. Woody said he had some things to do out in San Francisco and maybe he should go with them. He knew a ride they could get out of Philly with a friend of his who was, he said, a groovy spade, but they would have to let him know fast. Patsy phoned down to Philly, and while Woody was talking to his groovy spade friend, more people came in, many meetings were taking place, and Patsy was cooking broth for everyone. Some people who had been evicted brought their things in and rigged up their stereo tape set and started playing Chinese music. They had a TV set and they turned on a soap opera with the sound off. The sewing machine upstairs jangled the picture, zagging the people in half. A girl with freckles passed Patsy a joint. Everyone was full of peace, and Patsy was happy because they were. Then Peter Gone walked in.

Peter had been on speed for two weeks and for the last two days Patsy was the only person he could talk to and the only person he could bear to even look at. He cried, head down, his narrow bird shoulders slumped, his arms tight at his sides as he stood against her. They went into the bathroom to talk.

"Who are all those people?" he said. His eyes were gray. She had noticed they were getting grayer every day.

"They're good people, Peter. They're like you and me."

"Who was that big guy?"

"I don't know who you mean."

"The one ..." He shook his head. He couldn't go on.

"Peter, Peter, Peter," she said softly and put her arms around him. He put his face against her neck. Soon her neck was wet. She lifted his face, it was wet with tears, and she kissed him. She held him and kissed him a long time, not moving her face but gently kissing him again and again, and she felt him relaxing.

"Do you feel better?"

"A little."

"Do you want to lie down?"

"There's too many people."

"There's a place upstairs."

Patsy led Peter through the room, which was now much quieter than before, everyone was smoking and some were watching the people getting cut up on TV, and the stereo was playing sitar music. Woody was still on the phone to his friend in Philly.

The room where Patsy took Peter was two floors up, and two floors up it was another world. The long, brown and gray corridor was narrower than the other halls. The doors looked as if they hadn't been opened in years. Patsy wondered if the people who lived up here ever came out.

They went down the hall and Patsy glanced at Peter. His face was out of shape with an awful frown. It was dead white and crumpled into mean little lines. Suddenly he was a pitiful little old man years and years older than Mr. Moluska.

The room wasn't locked — there was no reason to lock it. It was small and bare — no bathroom, no closet, no sink. The only thing in the room was a small window in the outside wall. Patsy slowly shut the door behind them. She had brought a blanket, and she spread it on the floor. She sat down and held up her hand to Peter Gone. He looked down at her, his eyes gray and vacant. He stared at her as if he had just seen her, as if she had appeared out of nowhere and he was wondering where she came from, who she was. He slowly sat down beside her.

"I saw ..." he started, stopped, shook his head, his eyes clenched, his head hanging. Then he opened his eyes and quickly looked around, looked right at Patsy. "Do you know what I saw?"

"What did you see?"

"I was just going down the street and ... I saw ..." Again he stopped.

"You saw many things, didn't you, Peter?"

He stared at her a long time. "Eating," he whispered. "They were eating. Everyone was eating and I stood and looked at them. They just kept on eating and I stood on the sidewalk and watched them doing it."

"It's all right, Peter."

He was still staring at her, his eyes while she looked into them, seeming to become even grayer, as if deep within them a vortex was swirling, slowly and steadily emptying all the color out of him. "Poor baby," Patsy said, and kissed him.

She unbuttoned his jacket and started taking it off. He moved his arms, assisting her. She unbuttoned his shirt and took it off. His body was soft, small, and again Patsy thought of Mr. Moluska and his soft fat body: it occurred to her that Mr. Moluska carried another person around under his skin, a person like Peter. Maybe Mr. Moluska had absorbed a young man into himself, absorbed all but for one vital part of the young man which Mr. Moluska allowed to remain on the outside so he could use it on chickies.

Patsy pushed gently on Peter Gone and he lay back on the blanket. She took off her sweater and jeans while he stared up at her, his gray eyes large. She leaned over him, put the nipple of her left breast into his mouth, and he closed his eyes.

She left Peter in the room, asleep at last, and she went back downstairs. When he woke in the tiny gray room he would wonder where he was, he might even be scared — it might be . . . bad. But Patsy couldn't stay with him until he woke. He might sleep for two days.

Back in the apartment some people had left, some new ones had come, and in the middle of the room stood two big Negroes very elegant in black leather, posing with their hands on the hips of their skin-tight slacks. One of them looked coldly at Patsy as she came in. The look was imperious, murderous. She shivered and went straight to him. "Hi," she said.

He stared at her and his frown intensified by the tightening of his eyes.

"Hey, Patsy," it was Woody. "I was talking to my buddy in Philly and this chick and a guy started hassling me about who I am and where I'm calling from and what the number is and what the address is and who has the phone, who pays for it, so I told them I was at a pay phone and then it just cuts like dead, man, and I can't even get a dial tone, you know?" As he ended he was speaking up to the queen, who was a foot taller than he. The queen stared back at him without blinking.

"Well," Patsy said, "I'll have to let Russell know so he can get in a new line."

The people who had been evicted started moving their stuff out — one of them, a fat fellow in black pajamas and a Panama hat had found a new place. That was good, because Patsy was running out of the little packages for making broth — and then she discovered she was now in fact all out because while she was upstairs with Peter someone had walked out with the last of the little packages.

It was raining now and everyone except the two black queens lay looking out the windows. It was just a shower and then the sun came out and, now in the west, shone through the windows and people stripped down and went to sleep in the sun.

"What's your name?" One of the black queens stood looking down at Patsy. Maybe he was thinking of stepping on her.

"Patsy. What's your name?"

"Your hands are bleeding."

She smiled, held up her hand, and looked at her fingernails. She nodded. "I chew my fingernails. When I was a kid I guess I never got enough of it and ..."

"Russell say the headquarters gotta move outa here." He slowly lifted a hand and pointed a huge finger at her face. "He say you done."

The others had turned and were watching. "The headquarters are moving, Patsy?" someone asked.

"Russell always tells Bird McWilliams and Bird McWilliams tells me about any messages he has," Patsy answered, looking to the side, then up at the queen.

He stared down at her. "He say you done."

Patsy smiled. "Groovy. I'm done." She nodded her head brightly. "So Bird McWilliams will come and tell me. Okay?"

"No bird about it. You just get your ass out." He looked around at them. "All of you. Out."

"No," Patsy said, still smiling, though the smile was numb on her face and she calmly wondered if he would hit her or kick her, and she decided she would rather he hit her for if he did he would hit her face, but if he kicked her she knew he would kick her in a breast. But she knew she had no choice — he would kick her, and while she waited, telling herself she wouldn't close her eyes until she actually saw him starting to move, someone across the room spoke.

151

"Friend." That was all he said. They all turned and looked at him. He was a little guy with long red hair. In his Jockey shorts he sat cross-legged in the sun and he held a big black revolver. And he didn't say anything else, he just looked at the queen.

The queen squinted, his black face ascending in folds and lines, as if to shield him from the little black eye at the end of the gun barrel.

There was a long silence. They listened to the sewing machine upstairs.

The queen curled his lips back in a strange smile, looked down at Patsy — she smiled back at him — and a thin jet squirted from between his teeth and hit her face.

Not wiping her face, she nodded and said softly, "All right," and the queen turned slowly. He and the other one walked out the door and didn't shut it behind them.

"Paulie," the red-headed guy with the gun said. One of the others who still had his clothes on jumped up and crossed the room, paused at the door, and went out.

Several of them started talking all at once, but the guy with the gun said sharply, "Cool it," and they were silent again.

Paulie came back smiling broadly. "They're gone." The young man with the gun touched the barrel to his forehead in a salute and stuck it under a pile of clothes beside him.

Patsy got up and went over and kissed the red-headed guy. He told her his name was Phillip.

Then some girls came in with two big brown sacks of doughnuts. They were hard but good, and then it was raining again and everyone lay back and watched the gray rain streak the windows and soak the squares of cardboard that replaced the broken panes.

People were coming and going. The rain stopped, the sun was out again, and after the darkness of the shower it was as if this were the beginning of a new day. The sun shone against the windows and Patsy turned and while Phillip talked to her, his voice seeming to come from far away, she looked toward the windows and at the sky, and as she was facing the sun on the glistening panes something flashed by the window — white, quick, a large pale pillow with arms and legs stuck out at the corners — and Phillip was saying "... the other chicks ..." and she saw the flash just as he said other, the streak snipping between the syllables, and by the time he said chicks, Patsy heard the first surprised gasps and the first scream of a girl standing with her hand on the window sill, and then people were talking all at once — "Did you see that." "I saw it but what was it?" — and Patsy knew what it was, and the girl still standing there with her hand on the window sill also knew what it was before someone said that it was Peter Gone, and someone said low, "Groovy. Peter's gone," and they were silent, as if what he said was profound, or as if it were a tricky punch line that they had to repeat several times to themselves before they could laugh. Then they were freed from the long silence when a girl said, "It's not funny, man," and the girl who screamed when she first saw him, screamed again and turned and looked at Patsy across the room and said, "I saw him falling. I saw his face as he was falling. " Some went to the window and tried to look down at the sidewalk, and as they did, Patsy stood up and in spite of herself she wondered if he would be on the sidewalk or if he had reached the street, and frowning she shook her head. But she couldn't leave it alone, and as she stood behind those who got to the window first she knew that he had hit the curb, and she closed her eyes and took a deep breath, for to have hit the curb was worse, much worse. Then they were all leaving the apartment, crowding at the door, Patsy with them, and she heard the girl talking in a shrill, disbelieving tone, "I saw his face. His eyes were open. He was falling with his eyes open," and a guy was holding her arm and talking back at her, into her face, trying to talk over her, to blur out her words with his, saying over and over to her in a voice trying for calmness but instead achieving an almost pedantic seesawing, the tone of a parent or a teacher being patient, "All right, so cool it. It's unimportant, dig? It's unimportant," and as Patsy was pushed along with them out the door and down the hall toward the stairs she wanted to tell the guy — who was a bore, she decided, a really big bore — that maybe it was important. How did he know what was important and what wasn't?

There was a hassle with the police and Mr. Moluska, and then that night the phone was working again and Patsy turned it over to a long-legged skinny blond named Gracie who had just arrived from Berkeley.

Patsy went for a walk and met a couple of fellows and went with them to a very crowded party in a basement apartment. After most of the people had left, she and one of the fellows, Roy, lay staring up at a slowly revolving amber glass ball hanging from the ceiling. She cried and told Roy about Peter Gone. "He was such a beautiful little guy, you know?" she said.

"With that name he like had a hex on him," Roy said.

She talked about Peter for a long time and as she did she suddenly understood what she felt was a deep, sad mystery: Peter was beautiful — and because he was beautiful he had to do what he did. And the beauty justified what he did. Beauty justified everything. "Hold me," she whispered to Roy as the slow sweep of amber light moved over them, and he held her. "Mirrors watch people," she whispered. "One time that's what Peter told me," though he hadn't told her that at all. "Isn't that beautiful?"

"Heavy," Roy said.

They left the basement apartment and walked around for a while and went to an all-night place. They sat at the counter and watched the all-night freaks and weirdos, and Roy told Patsy about himself, talking about when he was a kid, and Patsy supposed he was trying to cheer her up but she couldn't get interested. She V'd her fingers, smiled sadly at Roy, got off her stool at the counter, and left.

With her head down she walked, now and then looking up at the black windows of buildings. She wondered if anyone was sitting at one of those dark windows looking out, seeing her.

"I am becoming someone too," she said out loud. "The least a person can do is be someone." And she liked that. It gave her the warm glow of bravery.

She walked until the massive, solid hulks of night were etched into patterns and shapes by gray that slowly spilled into the city from the east. The silence was rumpled more and more frequently by the indistinct, submerged sounds of machinery like giants slowly coming to life.

She saw a man standing on a street corner. As she walked toward him he didn't turn or even lift his head. He was small and wore a shapeless coat. He stood with his head down so far Patsy thought he had gone to sleep staring at his feet. She stopped beside him. She looked down at his feet, then up at what she could see of his face, blotched by a gray and black stubble. At first she thought his eyes were closed. But then she saw his eyelids were cracked, though she couldn't see the eyes under them.

"You looking for a place to sleep, friend? I know a place just up the street about two ..."

"Fuck off," he rasped.

"I just ..."

"Fuck off."

She crossed the street and on the other side looked back at him. He still stood there with his head down.

She walked for a couple of hours and then went back to the apartment building. The building was awake, morning noises and voices rattling down the halls as she climbed the stairs. She walked down the hall, but the door to the apartment was locked.

She stared at the scars and gouges in the door. She knocked lightly.

"Go away." It was a man's voice, muffled though familiar.

"Come back later," a girl said.

She went back to the stairs and sat on the top step. She put her head on her knees and soon she was in the gray whirl that could become either delirium or sleep, and she looked for Peter Gone and was sure he would come tumbling out of the gray billows and she was confident that now she would get the meaning — he would stand naked before her and with his unblinking gray eyes tell her all of the horror and beauty he had found, since now he knew everything. Smiling with his knowledge, he would turn her on . . .

But there was nothing. She slept but fitfully, waking at the sound of her own voice though she hadn't heard what she said and couldn't remember to whom she thought she was speaking. She slept again, and woke when she heard the apartment door being unlocked. Mr. Moluska came out wearing his gray suit and his wide-brimmed black felt hat. He was nodding and saying goodbye to someone in the apartment. Then he shut the door, turned, and saw Patsy. He tipped his hat. "How's Gracie?" Patsy said flatly.

"Fine. A little skinny but she's a good girl." As he passed her he patted her shoulder. "Bye-bye," he said and started down the stairs.

In the apartment Gracie, still naked, was talking on the phone. Patsy walked over to the windows and stood looking out.

"No . . . Listen ... 1 didn't mean that. Just. . . Listen. Do this. Tell him you'll do it if he'll pay some of the gas, tell him five bucks, that's not too

155

much ... I know, so he's a prick, but you'd be a prick too if . . . So just a chance give him a chance, okay? Is that asking too much for Chrissake?"

Patsy went to the door. "Hey, kid," Gracie said and Patsy turned. "Wait a minute, okay?"

Patsy smiled and shook her head.

Gracie shrugged her bony shoulders and went back to talking on the phone.

On the street again Patsy stood on a corner watching the cars glide along. A steady rumble throbbed in the streets, vibrating between the buildings. She walked down the street and around her pulsed the presence of people, and she stared at their faces, at their quick eyes, waiting for someone to look at her.

A SONG OF OLD FANGLES

HE RAN DOWN THE DARK CORRIDOR, whizzing by rooms where people lay like stones, though surely one or two were awake to see an angelic white blur — Hobart Stull! — fly by the door. On stat calls he reached wards faster than any house orderly in the history of Wichita Falls, and so he was a great favorite with the nurses. Most orderlies on eleven-to-seven hid out and slept. But Hobart wasn't interested in sleep as such. Young, a boy practically, just married and soon to be a father, he had curly hair, blue eyes and deep dimples in both cheeks — how could the nurses resist him? And those stately, monumental nurses, big and dour as battleships, adored him, revealing glimpses of large-motioned delicacy, ponderous heavy-fleshed girlishness, and a loamy femininity that made his head spin.

For them he performed heroics, defended them and protected a disturbed patient from himself by cajoling him into handing over a butcher knife he sneaked through admission. And it was Hobart Stull the ladies called to preserve dignity when they would discover a dead person lying in a bed on their ward, as if a vulgar trick had been pulled under their noses. They became stern and silent; sometimes they were nearly addled. Only death could ripple their placid control, like a bank of revelers howling across a lake in the middle of the night.

For the nurses there was an unhinged period between the discovery of the death and when Hobart came running to perform his duty, a time when everything might come loose — the doors flapping open and beds, chairs, people sailing out like big bats. Or if nothing came undone inside, the world outside might slide away — one looked out the nearest window for reassurance that the empty street, the store fronts across the way, were still there.

By and by a doctor, half-asleep, would arrive and spend two minutes in the room with the door closed; he would come out and write on the chart. Hobart would then remove the body. But after the bed had been quickly changed and the room thoroughly cleaned, there might linger a dawn-like expectancy, for death not always left with the dead person — and once Hobart thought he heard twangy steel music from another ward, or from the roof: music jagged with distance, but persistent, chewed with fade-outs and holes of silence in which he could almost hear whispers, laughter. It wasn't until a new patient had been admitted to the room and lay in the vacant bed, that the nurses again had full control.

Even dealing with the dead was an adventure for Hobart Stull, he was that young. Of course it lacked the glory of risking a knife wound, but something in him was satisfied when he took a body to the basement morgue and lugged it from the cart onto one of the long sliding trays that he would then ease into the large refrigerator. He later recalled standing beside the body of a man he had delivered to that place. The body lay densely physical, as if the flesh had become incalculably preoccupied. Without thinking, Hobart laid his hand on the man's arm. Hobart was urging him on.

He spent most of his time from eleven to seven sitting with the nurses who last called him to their ward. They made regular rounds of their patients, and if all was quiet, between times they were free. They talked and Hobart listened, usually. Their lives were complicated, for most of them had children who were grown and married. The happiness of their children's families seemed to slip through their fingers, but they always got a good hold on the strife. The nurses accepted their children's ordeals as personal challenges, and against even the grimmest, most boggling circumstances they charged into battles as dauntlessly as they would stride into a hospital room where the wolf breath of cancer hung in the air. Through the ordeals of their children's families they suffered as much as they had through their own — perhaps more, to hear them tell it. For there was just so much they could actually do. Sometimes they had to just "wait and see" — how often Hobart heard that. You might think that since they were old hands as nurses they would have realized there prevailed a downward inevitability in things, but Hobart saw in them no more acceptance or wisdom than in other people, and certainly less inclination to accepting defeat.

They were downright uncanny, sized up Hobart's moods as neatly as switching on a soap opera, and wouldn't let him be until he laid out all the trouble. Then he was counseled. Mrs. Nash was especially fine — she had a reputation even among the nurses for highpowered advice which she recited with the loveliest voice Hobart had ever heard. And she was huge. Her arms and legs bulged, and her hips were little people stowed away under her uniform, riding her through the night.

Mrs. Nash would light a cigarette, when she was sure no doctors were about and that the nurses' supervisor was off on another floor, and blowing a puff of smoke toward the low ceiling of the nursing station she would tell Hobart he shouldn't worry so much. She was sure Junie would make it through the last weeks of her pregnancy — and if Junie could, Hobart could. In fact, Mrs. Nash went on, Hobart could make it through anything! Why? "Because you're young and you're smart, Hobart," she said. "That's why."

"You're just half-right on that."

The other nurse at Mrs. Nash's station was large, though alongside Mrs. Nash she was just a rowboat. Hobart forgot nearly everything about her except there was in her family chronic strife. It clamped her in a very private silence. She had long ago refused Mrs. Nash's lyrical advice. While Mrs. Nash and Hobart talked, this other nurse stared down the dark corridor as if waiting for someone.

"No false modesty," Mrs. Nash told Hobart. "You can whip anything. You know what?" — she winked sending shivers through him as he stared at her face, small and coy atop her big body. "I can tell about people," she said and licked her lips.

He was sure later, just as he knew it then without letting himself think about it, that he and those nurses were making love. They were doing it as thoroughly as they could under the circumstances. With her soft voice Mrs. Nash would stir and lift Hobart. She analyzed refrigerator breakdowns and debated the virtues of retread tires, as Hobart sat before her on a little stool, his knees apart, looking like frog gone a-courting, and once Mrs. Nash leaned forward, looking Hobart straight in the eye, and knocked the wind out of him by putting a hand on his knee. While she recited the log of voyages to the Salvation Army and Chester's Tenth Street Thrift Store where, she guaranteed him, a young couple could find bins of like-new baby things, her hand went higher and squeezed his thigh. Then she leaned back, lit a cigarette, and blew smoke at the ceiling.

But sometimes right in the middle of listening to Mrs. Nash or one of the others, Hobart would look away for a moment and without meaning to he would slip away and in the familiar old nervous despair he would be worrying about Junie and the pregnancy and what all that would cost, for all he had to his silly name was $16. He was always alone.

He heard nothing as Mrs. Nash talked. He had to be there in that hospital all night. Had to wait all night before he could go back out and deal with all those problems ... No. They were worse than that. They were enemies that menaced what he presumptuously, innocently, with pitiful young-man naiveté called his family — a seventeen-year-old child and 8/9ths of a new child, hiding from winter night in a two-room apartment in a town gouged into the prairie of North Texas, and a pick-up truck a year older than Junie, worthless old pile of iron that half the time refused to start, and a refrigerator that regularly shorted out, ruining everything, and when it wasn't playing that game it nipped Junie (never Hobart) with cunning jolts that could, all three of them knew, any day bite big enough to swallow Junie, baby, everything. And Hobart already owed going on $300 to Junie's folks, friends, uncles, Mrs. Nash. . .

And while he sat up all night there in the hospital, his problems, those hunker-shouldered cretin enemies, were resting up for another day. And when seven o'clock came and Hobart could at last go out again, they would be waiting. Full of new schemes and meanness, they would be hiding out by his truck. And Hobart would head across the parking lot, exhausted, drained out, just flat numb and vulnerable, too helpless to do anything but say All hell, as they sprang screaming and howling from their ambush and fell on him like baboons.

"I can tell about people," Mrs. Nash confided, waking him. "Even strangers. It doesn't take forever to know people, and then you see that even before you knew them they weren't really strangers." Old lover, she smiled, made him smile back.

But on Five, the top floor of the hospital, Hobart didn't make love. When he was called up there he invariably found the nurses sitting in a tense, determined silence. He soon learned this didn't mean he had stepped onto an abruptly truced battlefield. A mood prevailed on Five which wasn't directly the doing of the nurses or the patients. But on Five Hobart could feel in the air the essence of the hospital: here people who had once been well and whole were waning — some going so far they wouldn't come back. Hobart sat up there in silence with the nurses, turning when he thought he heard something over the whir of ventilation blowers and the hum of florescent lights. . .

Five dogged him, followed him home and all the way to bed where, blindfolded with one of Junie's nylons, he tossed and turned, floundering in the lapping shallows, trying to make it out to where giant fish slowly roll and glide. And often he found himself back at the hospital listening to a talking garden, row on row of nurses. He would answer them over his shoulder while he hurriedly catheterized a patch of nodding cucumbers and in the next moment he dumped a wheelbarrow of cadavers rumbling down the chute of a potato bin. He woke shouting answers to the shadows of fish big as clouds.

And in that first moment he saw too clearly and the bedroom was loud. The sun then through the curtains shriveled those moments to gray runts that edged their way to the nearest corner and disappeared. And when Hobart tried to remember what had been so clear, so urgent, he could recall nothing. Except once he woke still seeing Mrs. Nash and some nurses sitting at the station on Five. In the rooms along the hall patients patted air. "They're finishing off," Mrs. Nash said, smiling coyly. The patients sank away, receding farther and farther into their rooms. "What is it now?" Hobart asked. "They're going off," she said, "to wide fields where there are no people and no familiar things."

And Junie burst into the room. "It's time!"

Hobart leaped from bed and stumbled around the room trying to find the door of the hospital. Junie jerked the stocking from his head and he got his pants on and a shirt, ran out and the truck amazingly started right up, and he drove Junie to the hospital. An orderly whisked her up to O.B., and Hobart went to the waiting room.

He paced for a couple of hours but had to sit down. He sat straight as a board, but he slept. They were in a bus station, there was no time to waste. Hobart was looking for Junie and at the same time talking to a young man who was following him around. The young man was Hobart's son!

Junie had no trouble delivering an eight-pound boy. They named him Hobart Stull, Jr. But a few months later Junie said he should have been named Dick Bunch, Jr. Hobart thought it over and decided he could live with that. But Junie couldn't. After she left, Hobart quit his job at the hospital, waited around a few weeks, and then left Wichita Falls. He set out to do a good job of turning over a leaf.

A VERY MODERN HOME

HELEN DROOSMAN'S DAUGHTER CAME HOME to have her baby and get her divorce. Naturally she brought her three little girls with her, Helen's precious granddaughters, rubber stamps of their mother. Two days later Helen had her stroke.

In the hospital Helen woke each morning believing she was in an empty house — for thirty years she had sold real estate. There were other obscurities. Time swiftly padded down the corridor in rubber-soled shoes, or the hours hung motionless like forgotten coats in a closet. Thought was tattered. Words flew through her mind like windblown scraps of paper playing chase in a house where all the windows were broken out. All this was to be expected, Helen was told. She wasn't worried, though she told herself — speaking out loud, which seemed to help — she told herself she *should be* worried. As she lay trying to think this through, ideas stumbled from each other's grasp and lurched down the corridor. What bothered her most was the irregularity of her memory — a radio in another room, sometimes blaring, sometimes so faint she barely heard it over the roar of silence.

But then Helen improved. One day at noon while she was eating a bowl of Jello, a giant's huge fingers snapped, sending a shockwave through her, and she was once again herself. "It's over now," she told her daughter Evie who came to visit that evening. "Everything's perfect now, Evie. Isn't that wonderful?"

The next morning Helen announced to her doctor "I'll live now, Doctor Nye." She laughed loudly, convincingly. The doctor, standing by her bed, patted her foot, smiled, and looked away. "Sure. You'll live a long time."

Helen convalesced at home for a month and then, against Dr. Nye's advice, returned to work. She had no choice — she had been on her own since the death of her husband Rudolph ten years ago. And now Evie had come to stay. Evie was busy being mother to those lovely little girls — she certainly couldn't go out and look for a job. And in her seventh month and her nerves completely shattered by the divorce ...

So Helen picked up where she had left off. Except her pace was slow, so slow Dr. Nye had nothing to worry about. She worked for a straight salary — she didn't drive herself for those commissions. She was at the real estate office each morning at nine, answered the phone, made all the sales meetings, and showed houses when no other agents were on hand.

And she promised herself she would never again go near the modem house on Twenty-eighth Street. She had been showing it when she had her stroke. A peculiar house, it had stood empty for several years waiting for a buyer. In Helen's slow, echoing dreams in the hospital, the house was a maze in which she searched for faces she had known years ago, following wisps of conversation that passed through the rooms like drafts of cold air.

Then almost by accident Helen made a sale. And another — that not by accident. She was back into it, and in two weeks had regained all the weight Dr. Nye made her lose, but she told herself it wasn't very noticeable, especially with Evie so big, into her eighth month ...

She did all the running around and endless telephoning necessary in closing the sales, and she was back to normal, she told herself, though she made silly mistakes which she tried to ignore, and though some days passed with an eerie slowness, and perhaps because of their slowness she was very forgetful on those days. Other times it took her by surprise: suddenly everything slid from her mind as if water were pouring over her head. But she was herself again, she insisted. Everything was fine.

Late one afternoon a couple came into the office. They were interested in seeing the unusual modern house advertised in the newspaper.

Helen happened to be the only agent in the office. And the commission on that sale would be a whopper. But thinking of the house gave Helen a queasy, sinking sensation, as if the office were slowly sliding downhill.

"One moment, please," she told the couple and went into the next cubicle. She picked up the phone to call another agent, Hank, home sick with a spring cold. Hank would have risen from his death bed to show that house. Helen's hand, reaching for the dial on the phone, hesitated. She stared at the fat little hand, the short, blunt fingers.

She put down the phone and went into her office. "I'll show the house," she said, smiling at the room.

She added, unable to stop herself, "But we'll have to wait until tomorrow."

The time was set and the couple left. Helen sat at her desk panting. She leaned back and wiped her forehead with a Kleenex. She was blinking rapidly — she put her hand over her eyes and made them close. "My," she said out loud. She tried to laugh. "My, my. What a silly girl."

That night she lay rigid in bed, her eyes closed, pretending she was sleeping. When she finally slept, she woke sitting straight up in bed, words still moving in the darkness. She laid back, her hands resting on her round stomach. Now she was afraid to sleep, but she passed into a silent, hollow dream that didn't free her until the watery gray light of dawn filled the room: Helen sat in a long, white room. Far away she heard solemn but jumbled words. Glancing around, she saw she was alone in the room. The funeral went on, static, interminable, and Helen sat in the pew talking to herself, her voice steady, droning, and after a while she realized the somber, incoherent words she heard far away were her own.

When Helen drove up in front of the house, just twenty minutes late, the couple who had come to the office yesterday weren't there.

Helen got out and went up the sidewalk to the house. They had probably left a note.

The mailbox was full of mail. Helen was taking the letters from the box when a woman opened the door. "Yes?" the woman said, looked at the mail in Helen's hands, then back at Helen and smiled. She was a lovely, slender, gray-haired lady. That was how Helen wished *she* looked. In fact, the woman reminded Helen of herself. Helen smiled at the lady, her mind fluttered with the thought that perhaps this slender, happy woman was herself . . .

"Is that your car going off by itself?" the lady asked pleasantly.

Helen turned and watched her car move smoothly down the street. With a solid thunk it nudged the bumper of a parked car, caromed, and, rolling on, lumbered over a curb and headed deliberately for a tree which it butted into and stopped.

"Oh my," Helen said. Water poured swiftly through her head. She lifted a hand. The hand pawed air, and Helen watched it. The plump, pale hand was all she could see.

She lay on a lovely chintz sofa in a lovely room. The lady's name was Mrs. Pugerel. Helen heard herself talking. "... and Evie who is just the sweetest thing when I dress her in those little pinafores ..."

She sat up and looked around. "What a lovely home," she said softly. "Such lovely gold sconces. And I just love the way they all harmonize, the walls, the gold molding along the ceiling. You wouldn't have trouble selling this house. I'm a real estate agent, did I tell you?"

Still talking, she rose. Mrs. Pugerel helped her with her coat and at the door Helen kissed Mrs. Pugerel's cheek. "You're such a dear," Helen said. "You look just like my Evie will look. I mean ..." She laughed and shook her head. "My."

On the steps they looked down the street, the trees new-leafed and motionless under a sky in which a few placid clouds hung as if they had been pinned there so everything would look just right.

Then Helen remembered. "Oh my. I can't understand how I missed that house. This is Twenty-eighth, isn't it?"

"No, dear," Mrs. Pugerel said. "This is Forty-fifth."

"Oh. That explains everything. You know, Dr. Nye told me ... I believe I will start carrying a little notebook with me at all times. Dr. Nye said I could expect ... and I'm beginning to think he was right." She laughed. "I tend to be a little forgetful. I will be that way for a while. Do you know Dr. Nye?"

Mrs. Pugerel was inside and slowly shutting the door.

Helen walked carefully down the sidewalk and angled across the street to her car. Some children stood by the car. "Back away, kiddies. This will be dangerous. That tree might fall over when I back up." She glanced up the sloping lawn of the house whose tree her car had struck. The windows, reflecting the sky, stared blankly.

She got in the car, started it, and gripping the steering wheel, shut her eyes after giving the tree one last look. She raced the motor and backed away. She opened her eyes to see the tree still standing.

Helen swung out into the street and she had driven several blocks when the screaming voice of a child came looming from behind her. Had she heard the scream when she backed away from the tree? Had she in fact *heard* a scream?

"Oh my." She stopped the car, pulled into the driveway, and turned around. But she couldn't find the street — Was it Twenty-fifth? Thirty-third . . .

She drove up and down looking at the houses sternly lining the streets, and each time she approached boys and girls playing she slowed the car almost to a stop, staring at them, while the children looked back at her.

She drove into the afternoon, no longer looking for the house with the tree, no longer stopping at each group of children. She drove on and on until, as though of its own accord, her car stopped at the curb in front of the small house on Logan Avenue where she and Rudolph had lived for thirty years.

That night after the little ones were in bed, Helen and Evie sat in the front room watching TV. Helen was talking and all at once she came quite close, for just a moment, to remembering something important from that afternoon. It involved death ... Maybe on the late news ...

When the news came on, she watched closely, not talking, but the news concerned the affairs of people far away. She watched the screen, nodding, and she was talking to Rudolph and Evie, and Helen watched herself rise and hurry out to the kitchen to get bowls of ice cream, and Evie was a little girl, and the three of them were talking and laughing while Helen watched, her lips puffing as she snored.

She woke in bed the next morning, opened her eyes, shut them, and saw the modern house on Twenty-eighth: gray, with massive square hunks of concrete boxed together like the building blocks of a giant child. She tried to forget the house, but it had moved into her and become not just a part of memory, but memory itself: the large white rooms where faces and voices become the past.

In the afternoon Mr. and Mrs. Taylor, the couple interested in seeing the house, met Helen at the office. Helen started to apologize for missing them yesterday, but *they* apologized to *her.* Mr. Taylor yesterday had been called out of town at the last minute.

So they loaded into Helen's car, and chatted as they drove along.

The Taylors were an interesting couple — maybe just the people to buy that house. Drake Taylor was rather impatient and nervous. He wore a little black hat, and craftily arched his brows, intently staring at Helen as she talked. Mrs. Taylor, pale and slender, laughed often and forcefully, stopping abruptly, expressionless, as if she hadn't laughed at all. She reminded Helen of Evie. Helen asked if they had children. "Yes," Taylor answered. "As my wife said, we have a daughter."

"Oh, yes," Helen said as if she remembered having been told. "How wonderful. Children are such a pleasure. Our Evie has been such a pleasure to Rudolph and me. And now her children, our little granddaughters …"

The day was exceedingly bright. Houses along the street shone in the sunlight, and the trees held themselves rigid, as if their brilliant leaves were glass.

"Have you lived here long?" Helen asked.

Taylor, riding in the front seat, looked out the window. Mrs. Taylor answered from the back seat: "We're moving here."

"Oh, yes. That's right," Helen said.

She drove on, talking rapidly. She interrupted herself to ask Mr. Taylor if he had happened to see a Euclid Avenue street sign.

"Back there," Taylor said low.

"Oh dear." Helen turned the car — making an approaching car swerve to miss them, its tires squealing. "People drive too fast," Helen muttered. She went on talking.

"There," Taylor said loudly.

"What?"

"Euclid."

"Oh. Well. We can … turn around."

"This is utterly …" Taylor started but Mrs. Taylor, leaning forward, cut him off with shrill laughter. "I do the same thing all the time," Mrs. Taylor said loudly.

Not talking, Helen carefully circled the block and got on Euclid.

"The house is on Twenty-seventh?" Taylor asked. Helen nodded. "Then it should be right up here," he said. "Twenty- seventh," he repeated slowly.

Helen nodded. "Twenty-seventh. Twenty-seventh."

"There!" Taylor said.

They made the turn.

"Now," Helen said. The Taylors sat back in their seats. "All the houses on this street are very modern. If you like modern houses, this is the house for you, and this is the neighborhood for you. Now here you see some of the modern designs." Taylor was looking out his window. He grunted.

"Now let me see ..." Helen said, slowing the car. "1604 ..."

"Up there," Taylor said.

They stopped in front of 1604, an English Tudor. There wasn't a for sale sign in the front yard. The motor idled and they stared at the house. "I don't think this ..." Mrs. Taylor said cautiously.

"This obviously isn't the right street," Taylor said.

"Let me see ..." Helen dug into her big purse. "I put the address and all the information ... Here." She pulled out a note card. At the top was written in the precise script of Helen's hand before her stroke, "Reminder!" The rest of the card and the other side were blank.

"Well? Is that it?" Taylor asked.

"I don't think so," Helen said and stuck the card back into her purse.

"This is a waste of time," Taylor said. "Why don't we ..."

"Drake," Mrs. Taylor said, her voice rising until it trilled. into sharp laughter. "Let's try one street over."

Helen let out the clutch and the car lurched forward. They turned one corner, then the second, and as soon as they did, Helen felt water pouring over her head. Her arms became tremendously heavy and she gripped the wheel. She drove slowly down Twenty-eighth street. Her mouth was dry, her tongue thick. "I don't want ..." she started, but choked. She tried to swallow. Finally all she could do was smile slightly.

At 1604 they found what at first glance was an enormous empty lot covered with trees and underbrush. But through the tangled landscaping gone wild they saw a high gray wall. The bushes at one time had probably been neatly trimmed; now they sprawled, grappling with one another. In the center of the trees lurked a leafless spine, a tree naked and guilty of death. A weed-clotted stone walk, with some steps missing, disappeared into the bushes and trees.

"Is this it?" Taylor said low.

Helen didn't answer.

"It's ... *marvelous*," Mrs. Taylor whispered.

"Hmm," Taylor said. "I think I like it."

They got out and started up the walk. Taylor helped Helen and Mrs. Taylor where the stepping stones were missing. The earth was gouged and scarred in these places, and Helen recognized the narrow curlicue roads of children's toy cars.

At the top they confronted the wall. Helen walked to one end, then the other while Mr. and Mrs. Taylor stood staring up it toward the sky. "There's no door," Helen muttered. "No door."

"Around the side," Taylor said. "It's on the other side."

"Yes," Helen said vaguely. Then emphatically, "Yes."

They followed a narrow path made either by children or dogs. High in the side wall, narrow vertical windows were cut in rows corresponding to the several storeys of the house.

"Isn't this marvelous?" Mrs. Taylor said.

"It's modern," Helen said, her head down.

At the opposite end of the house another nearly impenetrable screen of trees and brush concealed a high blank wall. The Taylors backed into the bushes to appreciate the wall, while Helen walked along it.

"The door is around the corner," Taylor said confidently and led the way. Upon turning the corner they stood above what at first seemed a ravine but was in fact a driveway burrowed under the house.

"Oh," Helen said. "Yes. We go in through the garage door." She smiled. "See, I was right. There really isn't a door. Not a real door. Everyone goes in through the garage."

"I don't like that," Taylor said.

"Let's see it all before we decide what we like and don't like," Mrs. Taylor said.

Taylor led them down to the driveway.

Cut into rock beside the garage door was an oval steel hatch. Helen unlocked it and pushed with both hands. It swung open with a creak, and they stared into darkness.

Taylor dauntlessly stepped forward. He reached around the corner for a light switch but found none. Without hesitating, he disappeared through the door.

He was gone a minute, two, longer. Mrs. Taylor stuck her head in the door and called, "Drake? Isn't there a light somewhere?"

At that moment a light came on inside and Mrs. Taylor and Helen stepped into a white tile tunnel glistening under a blaze of lights.

"A big, roomy garage," Helen said uncertainly. "Very nice."

"It's the entrance way," Taylor said from atop a spiral staircase high above them. "The garage is back there."

Helen and Mrs. Taylor carefully climbed the staircase, and the three of them entered what reminded Helen of a hatbox. "Isn't this interesting," Helen said.

Next, the kitchen — glass, aluminum, glaring tile. "I *love* this kitchen," Mrs. Taylor responded. "I simply *love* it."

Into more rooms — high ceilinged, gleaming white, large rooms, small rooms that weren't actually rooms but junctions of angling passageways connecting room clusters, and more rooms, some windowless, some sliced with rigid vertical windows high in the walls. "Why, there's no *end* to the rooms," Mrs. Taylor said.

"We're climbing," Taylor said eagerly. "The corridor is on an incline. We're climbing to the second floor." To Helen: "How many floors are there?"

Helen didn't answer, puffing, trying to keep up with them as they passed through room after identical room.

On the third floor the corridor forked. "Is there no *end* to this house!" Mrs. Taylor said faraway, and Helen whispered, "No," and followed to the right, walking along a wall and looking up its severe height toward the sky beyond the windows.

Helen paused in the next room. If only there were a chair where she could sit for a moment. Or any kind of furniture — it would help so much if only there were some furniture she could look at. But the room was immaculately bare, and as Helen stared across the large room she realized the far wall was glass, dull silvery gray. She crossed the room, her heels thumping loudly, hollowly, and stood before the wall. Her reflection was imperfect, and she couldn't see through the wall into the next room. "Isn't that interesting," she whispered, and wasn't surprised when neither Taylor nor his wife replied — they must have gone the other way when the corridor forked. Then in the glass wall Helen saw a woman looking out at her. "My," Helen said. She wondered if the woman was herself. Helen lifted her

171

hand — and the woman inside the glass lifted hers, but higher, as if she were reaching for Helen's head. The thought calmly entered Helen's mind that if there was no door in the wall, the woman couldn't leave. Squinting, she leaned closer. Dark swirls in the glass prevented her from seeing the woman clearly and from getting more than a vague impression of the room. It was a huge room, the largest she had ever seen. "My goodness," Helen said.

She turned and called out, "Evie?" Her voice returned slowly from the wall.

In another room the Taylors, talking eagerly, joined Helen. She nodded, though she didn't hear a word.

"Excuse me." She walked past them through the door. She turned right, then left at the next fork, hurrying. She looked in a room, said low, "Evie?" then went on down the corridor.

"Evie is at home," Helen said softly and nodded. "At home with Rudolph."

She turned back. Taylor was talking to her. She stared at his nose. It was quite large. His dark eyes were pulsing. "Aren't you feeling well?" Mrs. Taylor said into Helen's ear. Helen turned to her. "I didn't know you were there," Helen said, smiling. Mrs. Taylor's face was beautiful, soft, without lines, the face of a married woman in that time of life when there is beauty in everything that happens. "Do you have children?" she asked Mrs. Taylor.

They went on, Taylor talking, gesturing as he walked ahead, turning to make a point and glance at Helen and his wife.

"You have got us lost, Drake," Mrs. Taylor said, laughing pleasantly.

Helen walked away. After a while she stopped before a high white wall. She touched it, and it was cold. High, high above was the dim line where the wall touched the ceiling.

"Evie," she called and turned. Her voice bounced back sharply across the room and became louder with each brittle reverberation.

Walking between Mr. and Mrs. Taylor, Helen passed down a corridor. As Taylor talked he lifted both hands, palms up, as if lifting air. "How long have you been married to him?" Helen asked Mrs. Taylor.

At another fork the three went separate directions — Mrs. Taylor slowly walked up an incline, looking over her shoulder at Helen; Taylor turned and walked down the incline, looking up at his wife with a strained, quizzical expression; and before Helen took the other fork, she waved goodbye to them. She soon found herself before a high white wall, cold, and she looked up it to the line where the wall touched the ceiling. "Evie," she whispered and turned to hear her voice scuttling along the walls.

The Taylors came toward her down a wide incline, walking arm in arm and taking mincing steps. The couple was chatting silently. Helen knew they were far away and, though walking steadily with their rapid mincing steps, they weren't nearing Helen.

She started toward them, then, turning, she saw many doorways, more than she could count at a glance, lining both sides of a corridor. Slowly she sat on the white floor, tugging the hems of her coat and dress well below her knees and holding her purse on her lap. "My," she sighed. Her hands trembled. She caught her left wrist and tried to check her pulse. Maybe some aspirins. She dug into her purse and came out with a photograph of Rudolph, Evie, and herself, a picture taken when Evie was five years old. As she looked at it, the glare from the walls glinted on the shiny surface of the snapshot and abruptly they were gone and the house in the picture wasn't the little place on Logan Avenue in the summer of 1950, but a property for sale on the east side of town.

Naked, lean as a tree limb with its bark peeled away, Helen descended to sharp-angled, clicking corridors and doorways, a cold wind guiding her straight to Drake Taylor who stood, feet apart, beside his wife, his expression suspicious. As Helen approached, Mrs. Taylor backed away. Helen lifted her arms — they were young and thin and very long — and she put them around Drake Taylor's neck. Not closing her eyes, she kissed him and they floated back, going faster and faster, Drake Taylor beneath her, his eyes open, deep brown, serious, thinking the things a man thinks. Helen told herself she was Mrs. Taylor. "I will be her this once," Helen whispered. "But just once. I won't do it again, promise."

Not looking back, Helen left them. She would find herself.

A smooth wall revolved and Helen walked along it. She stopped before turning a corner and waited a moment. Then, prepared, she turned the corner to see what she knew she must see.

Helen Droosman, fat lady, lay on her back, her coat unbuttoned, the toes of her shoes pointing out.

Several young men bent over her, talking. One put his hands under her shoulders. Another gripped her ankles. They lifted her fat little body onto a stretcher. She heard them grunting.

They paused, stood, talked again.

Then they lifted the stretcher and their hollow footsteps echoed down the corridor. Helen heard one of them speak and the others chuckled. Their footsteps were now far away. A muffled bump carried down the corridors and through the rooms. Then silence.

Helen turned and immediately Mrs. Taylor came out of a room, speaking over her shoulder. From the same room came Taylor and then Helen, herself, her head bobbing in agreement as she listened to Mrs. Taylor. The three of them came down the corridor silently, though still talking, and it appeared all three spoke at once, nodded in unison, paused for a moment, then Taylor went on talking, gesturing with both hands. The three of them passed Helen and went on down the corridor. Helen went the other way.

Upstairs, she wandered through the white rooms. In the corner of a room she found a staircase and she climbed to the top floor of the house. There, in three small rooms, the windows were low enough for her to see out.

She saw clear across town, houses nearly hidden by trees, large buildings downtown.

Late in the afternoon Mr. and Mrs. Taylor and Helen climbed the stairs to the top floor and went through the three rooms, talking silently, each looking once quickly out the windows but concentrating on the rooms. Then they went back downstairs.

Far below, near the house, Helen heard the faint voices of children playing. She tried to look down the steep wall, but she couldn't see them.

The sun set swiftly and darkness slipped across town, hiding houses beneath trees meshed into a dark veil torn by streetlamps and dimmer, yellow light in the windows of homes.

Then it was night.

Helen stood by the window, waiting. Tomorrow would be her second day. But in a sense it would be her first.

Jerry Bumpus taught creative writing 35 years in Japan, China, and at six American universities, ending at San Diego State University. He and his wife, Bettie, live with their daughter, Margot, in Arlington, Virginia.

Acknowledgments

"Anaconda Excerpt" appeared in the novel *Anaconda* published by *December Magazine*, 1967.

"Things in Place" and "Patsy O'Day in the World" and "A Song of Old Fangles" appeared in the story collection *Things in Place* published by FICTION COLLECTIVE NEW YORK, 1975.

"Lovers" appeared in *Vagabond*, 1976

"Mrs. Bell and Her Dog", "House-Hunting Near the Frontier", "The Angel Business", "A Very Modern Home" are from the story collection *Special Offer*, Carpenter Press, Columbus, Ohio, 1981.

"A Lament to Wolves" is from *The Civilized Tribes New and Selected Stories*, The University of Akron Press, Akron, Ohio, 1995.

"Flowers in Your Hair" was published in *Rio Grande Review*, U. of Texas, El Paso, 1991.

"Dawn of the Flying Pigs" and "Mr. Tangible" appeared in the story collection *Dawn of the Flying Pigs*, Carpenter Press, Columbus, Ohio, 1992.

"Heroes and Villains" and "Chums" appeared in the story collection *Heroes and Villains*, FICTION COLLECTIVE NEW YORK, 1986.

www.ingramcontent.com/pod-product-compliance
Lightning Source LLC
Chambersburg PA
CBHW050744250626
47155CB00005B/1917